KB085200

중국인 거리

아시아에서는 《바이링궐 에디션 한국 대표 소설》 을 기획하여 한국의 우수한 문학을 주제별로 엄선해 국내외 독자들에게 소개합니다. 이 기획은 국내외 우수한 번역가들이 참여하여 원작의 품격을 최대한 살렸습니다. 문학을 통해 아시아의 정체성과 가치를 살피는 데 주력해 온 아시아는 한국인의 삶을 넓고 깊게 이해하는 데 이 기획이 기여하기를 기대합니다.

Asia Publishers presents some of the very best modern Korean literature to readers worldwide through its new Korean literature series 〈Bi-lingual Edition Modern Korean Literature〉. We are proud and happy to offer it in the most authoritative translation by renowned translators of Korean literature. We hope that this series helps to build solid bridges between citizens of the world and Koreans through a rich in-depth understanding of Korea.

바이링궐 에디션 한국 대표 소설 011

Bi-lingual Edition Modern Korean Literature 011

Chinatown

오정희

중국인 거리

Oh Jung-hee

ASIA PUBLISHERS

Contents

중국인 거리

Chinatown

시를 남북으로 나누며 달리는 철도는 항만의 끝에 이르러서야 잘려졌다. 석탄을 싣고 온 화차는 자칫 바다에 빠뜨릴 듯한 머리를 위태롭게 사리며 깜짝 놀라 멎고 그 서슬에 밑구멍으로 주르르 석탄가루를 흘려 보냈다.

집에 가 봐야 노루 꼬리만큼 짧다는 겨울해에 점심이 기다리고 있는 것도 아니어서 우리들은 학교가 파하는 대로 책가방만 던져 둔 채 떼를 지어 선창을 지나 항만의 북쪽 끝에 있는 제분 공장에 갔다.

제분 공장 볕 잘 드는 마당 가득 깔린 멍석에는 늘 덜 건조된 밀이 널려 있었다. 우리는 수위가 잠깐 자리를 비운 틈을 타서 마당에 들어가 멍석의 귀퉁이를 밟으며 한

Railroad tracks ran west through the heart of the city, dead-ending near a flour mill at the north end of the harbor. When a coal train jerked to a stop there, the locomotive recoiled as if in fear of dropping into the sea, sending coal dust trickling through chinks in the floors of the cars.

There was no lunch waiting for us at home on those winter days short as a deer's tail, so we threw aside our book bags as soon as school was over and flocked past the pier to the flour mill. The straw mats that covered the south yard of the mill were always strewn with wheat drying in the sun. If the custodian was away from his post at the front gate,

움큼씩 밀을 입안에 털어 넣고는 다시 걸었다. 올올이 흩어져 대글대글 이빨에 부딪치던 밀알들이 달고 따뜻한 침에 의해 딱딱한 껍질을 불리고 속살을 풀어 입안 가득 풀처럼 달라붙다가 제법 고무질의 질긴 맛을 낼 때쯤이면 철로에 닿기 마련이었다.

우리는 밀껌으로 푸우푸우 풍선을 만들거나 침목 사이에 깔린 잔돌로 비사치기를 하거나 전날 자석을 만들기 위해 선로 위에 얹어 놓았던 못을 뒤지면서 화차가 닿기를 기다렸다.

드디어 화차가 오고 몇 번의 덜컹거림으로 완전히 숨을 놓으면 우리들은 재빨리 바퀴 사이로 기어들어 가 석탄가루를 훑고 이가 벌어진 문짝 틈에 갈퀴처럼 팔을 들이밀어 조개탄을 후벼내었다. 철도 건너 저탄장에서 밀차를 밀며 나오는 인부들이 시꺼멓게 모습을 나타낼 즈음이면 우리는 대개 신발주머니에, 보다 크고 몸놀림이 잽싼 아이들은 시멘트 부대에 가득 석탄을 안고 낮은 철조망을 깨금발로 뛰어넘었다.

선창의 간이 음식점 문을 밀고 들어가 구석 자리의 테이블을 와글와글 점거하고 있으면 그날의 노획량에 따라 가락국수, 만두, 찐빵 등이 날라져 왔다.

we would walk in, help ourselves to a handful of wheat, leave a footprint on the corner of the mat, and be on our way. The wheat grains clicked against our teeth, and after the tough husks had steeped in our warm, sweet saliva, the kernels emerged, sticking like glue everywhere inside our mouths. By the time we reached the railroad they were good and chewy.

While we waited for the coal train we blew big bubbles with our wheat gum, set up rocks we had gathered from the roadbed and threw pebbles at them, or hunted for nails we had set on the rails the previous day to make magnets.

Eventually the train appeared, rattling to a stop with one last wheeze. We scurried between the wheels, raked up the coal dust, then hooked our arms through the gaps in the doors and scooped out some of the egg-shaped briquettes. Usually, by the time the carters from the coal yard across the tracks had made their dusty appearance, we had filled our school-slipper pouches with coal—the bigger and faster children used cement bags. Then, pouches and bags nestled beneath our arms, we hopped over the low wire fence on the harbor side of the tracks.

석탄은 때로 군고구마, 딱지, 사탕 따위가 되기도 했다. 어쨌든 석탄이 선창 주변에서는 무엇과도 바꿀 수 있는 현금과 마찬가지라는 것을 우리는 알고 있었고, 때문에 우리 동네 아이들은 사철 검정 강아지였다.

해안촌 혹은 중국인 거리라고도 불리는 우리 동네는 겨우내 북풍이 실어나르는 탄가루로 그늘지고, 거무죽죽한 공기 속에 해는 낮달처럼 희미하게 걸려 있었다.

할머니는 언제나 짚수세미에 아궁이에서 긁어낸 고운 재를 묻혀 번쩍 광이 날 만큼 대야를 닦았다. 아버지의 와이셔츠만을 따로 빨기 위해서였다. 그러나 바람을 들이지 않는 차양 안쪽 깊숙이 넌 와이셔츠는 몇 번이고 다시 헹구어 푸새를 새로 하지 않으면 안 되었다.

망할 놈의 탄가루들. 못 살 동네야.

할머니가 혀를 차면 나는 으레 나올 뒤엣말을 받았다.

광석천이라는 냇물에서는 말이다. 물론 난리가 나기 전 이북에서지. 빨래를 하면 희다 못해 시퍼랬지. 어느 독이 그렇게 퍼렇겠니.

겨울방학이 끝나면 담임인 여선생은 중국인 거리에 사는 아이들을 불러 학교 숙직실로 데리고 갔다. 그리고 숙직실 부엌 바닥에 웃통을 벗겨 엎드리게 하고는 미지근한

Our next stop was the snack bar on the pier, where we swarmed to the corner table. Depending on the day's plunder, our coal earned us noodle soup, wonton, steamed buns filled with red bean jam, edibles of that sort. Other times we swapped for baked sweet potatoes, picture cards, or candy. Coal was as good as cash—something we could trade for anything around the pier—and so the children in our neighborhood looked like black puppies year round.

Our neighborhood was Seashore Village to some, while others called it Chinatown. The coal dust carried in by the winter northerlies settled over the area like a shadow, blackening the sky and leaving the orb of the sun looking more like the moon.

Grandmother used to scoop ash from our stove, apply it to a fistful of straw, and polish the washbasin to a sparkling sheen before doing Father's dress shirts. But even though she hung the shirts to dry well inside the canopy, away from the dusty wind, she had to rinse them again and again and starch them a second time before she'd let him wear them.

"Damned coal dust! What a place to live!" Grandmother clucked.

물을 사정없이 끼얹었다. 귀 뒤, 목덜미, 발가락, 손톱 사이까지 탄가루가 없는 것을 확인하고서야 왕소름이 돋은 등허리를 찰싹찰싹 때리는 것으로 검사를 끝냈다. 우리는 킬킬대며 살비듬이 푸르르 떨어지는 내의를 머리부터 뒤집어 썼다.

봄이 되자 나는 삼 학년이 되었다. 오전반이었기 때문에 한낮인 거리를 치옥이와 나는 어깨동무를 하고 천천히 걸어 집으로 돌아오고 있었다.

나는 커서 미용사가 될 거야.

삼거리의 미장원을 지날 때 치옥이가 노오란 목소리로 말했다.

회충약을 먹는 날이니 아침을 굶고 와야 해요. 선생의 지시대로 치옥이도 나도 빈속이었다. 공복감 때문일까, 산토닌을 먹었기 때문일까, 해인초 끓이는 냄새 때문일까, 햇빛도, 지나다니는 사람들의 얼굴도, 치마 밑으로 펄럭이며 기어드는 사나운 봄바람도 모두 노오랬다.

길의 양켠은 가건물인 상점들을 빼고는 거의 빈터였다. 드문드문 포격에 무너진 건물의 형해가 썩은 이빨처럼 서 있을 뿐이었다.

제일 큰 극장이었대.

A certain reminiscence invariably followed. I heard it so often I could recite it in her place: "Let me tell you about the water from Kwangsŏk Spring. Now this was in the North before the war, you understand. With that water the wash turned out so white it seemed almost blue! Even lye couldn't get it that white."

When we returned to school after winter vacation our homeroom teacher took all us Chinatown children to the kitchen next to the night-duty room. There she made us strip to the waist, assume a pushup position on the floor, and endure a merciless dousing with lukewarm water. Then she checked for coal dust behind our ears, on the backs of our necks, between our toes and under our fingernails. An affectionate slap where the gooseflesh had erupted in the small of our backs meant we had passed inspection. We giggled as we slipped on our longjohn tops flecked with dead skin.

Spring arrived and with it the new school year. I was now a third-grader. My homeroom had classes only in the morning, and early one afternoon I was on my way home with Ch'i-ok, our arms around each other's shoulders.

"I'm going to be a hairdresser when I grow up,"

조명판처럼, 혹은 무대의 휘장처럼 희게 회칠이 된 한쪽 벽만 고스란히 남아 서 있는 건물을 가리키며 치옥이가 소곤거렸다. 그러나 그것도 곧 무너질 것이다. 나란히 들어선 인부들이 곡괭이의 첫 날을 댈 위치를 가늠하고 있었다. 어느 순간 희고 거대한 벽은 굉음으로 주저앉으리라.

한쪽에서는 이미 헐어 낸 벽에서 상하지 않은 벽돌과 철근을 발라내고 있는 중이었다.

아주 쑥밭을 만들어 버렸다니까.

치옥이는 어른들의 말투를 흉내 내어 몇 번이고 쑥밭이라는 말을 되풀이했다.

사람들은 개미처럼, 열심히 집을 지어 빈터를 다스렸다. 반 자른 드럼통마다 조개탄을 듬뿍 써서 해인초를 끓였다.

치옥이와 나는 자주 멈춰서서 찍찍 침을 뱉어 냈다.

회충이 약을 먹고 지랄하나 봐.

아냐, 회충이 오줌을 싸는 거야.

그래도 메스꺼움은 가라앉지 않았다. 끓어오르는 해인초의 거품도, 조개탄에서 피어오르는 연기도, 해조와 뒤섞이는 석회의 냄새도 온통 노란빛의 회오리였다.

Ch'i-ok said as we passed a beauty shop at a three-way intersection.

Her voice reminded me of yellow. It was worm-medicine day at school and we'd been instructed to arrive on an empty stomach. I wasn't sure if it was my hunger, the medicine, or the smell of boiling Corsican weed, but everything looked yellow—the sunlight, the faces of passersby, the gusts that crept under my skirt and set it aflutter.

Except for several makeshift stores and the occasional skeleton of a bombed-out building sticking out like a decaying tooth, both sides of the street were barren.

"It was supposed to be the biggest theater in town," Ch'i-ok whispered as she pointed out the one remaining wall of a ruined building. Plastered in white, it resembled a movie screen or the curtain of a stage. But not for long. A work crew were taking aim at it with pickaxes and in no time the great white wall would come roaring to the ground.

Other workers were removing the reusable bricks and reinforcing rods from a wall already demolished.

"The area was bombed to kingdom come," Ch'i-ok said, mimicking the adults and repeating "to king-

왜 사람들은 집을 지을 때 해인초를 쓰지? 난 저 냄새만 맡으면 머리털 뿌리까지 뽑히는 것처럼 골치가 아파.

치옥이는 내 어깨에 엇갈린 팔을 무겁게 내려뜨렸다. 그러나 나는 마냥 늑장을 부리며 천천히 걸어 해인초 냄새, 내가 이 시와 나눈 최초의 악수였으며 공감이었던 그 노란빛의 냄새를 들이마셨다.

우리 가족이 이 도시로 이사를 온 것은 지난해 봄이었다.

늬 아버지가 취직만 되면……. 어머니는 차곡차곡 쌓은 담뱃잎에 푸우푸우 입에 가득 문 물을 뿜는 사이사이 말했다. 담뱃잎을 꼭꼭 눌러 담은 부대에 멜빵을 해서 메고 첫새벽에 나가는 어머니는 이틀이나 사흘 후 초죽음이 되어 돌아오곤 했다.

간이 열이라도 담배 장사는 이제 못 해먹겠다. 단속이 여간 심해야지. 늬 아버지 취직만 되면…….

미리 월남해서 자리를 잡았거나 전쟁을 재빨리 벗어난 친구, 동창들을 찾아다니며 취직 운동을 하던 아버지가 석유 소매 업소의 소장직으로 취직을 하고, 우리를 실어 갈 트럭이 온다는 날 우리는 새벽밥을 지어 먹고 이불 보따리와 노끈으로 엉글게 동인 살림도 구들을 찻길에 내다 놓았다. 점심때가 되어도 트럭은 오지 않았다. 한없이 길

dom come" over and over.

Diligent as ants, the residents had reclaimed the devastated areas and were rebuilding their houses. Pots of Corsican weed boiled on heaps of coal briquettes in stoves made from oil drums.

Ch'i-ok and I constantly stopped to spit big gobs of saliva.

"Feels like the worms took the medicine and went nuts."

"Uh-uh, I think they're peeing."

Whatever it was they were doing, it didn't make us any the less nauseated. The froth from the Corsican weed, the smoke from the coal, and the odor of plaster combined with the seaweed smell of the Corsican weed were one big yellow whirl.

"I wonder why they use Corsican weed when they're building a house," Ch'i-ok said. "One whiff and I get a splitting headache."

The arm looped around my shoulder dropped like a dead weight. I dawdled along, drinking in the smell of the Corsican weed. That yellow smell had been my introduction to this city, the very first understanding I shared with it.

My family had moved here the previous spring

게 되풀이되는 동네 사람들과의 작별 인사도 끝났다.

해질 무렵이 되자 어머니는 땅뺏기놀이나 사방치기에도 진력이 나 멍청히 땅바닥에 주저앉은 우리들을 일으켜 세워 읍내의 국수집에서 국수를 한 그릇씩 사 먹였다. 집을 나서기 전 갈아입은 옷이건만 한없이 흐르는 콧물로 오빠와 나 그리고 동생은 소매와 손등이 반들반들하게 길이 들었다.

날이 완전히 어두워졌어도 어머니는 젖먹이를 안고 이불 보따리 위에 올라앉은 채 트럭이 나타날 다릿목께만을 뚫어지게 노려보고 있었다.

트럭이 나타난 것은 저물고도 한참이 지난 후였다. 헤드라이트를 밝힌 트럭이 요란한 엔진 소리와 함께 다릿목에 모습을 드러내자 어머니는 차가 왔다, 라고 비명을 질렀다. 저마다 보따리 하나씩을 타고 앉았던 우리 형제들은 공처럼 튀어 일어났다. 트럭은 신작로에서 잠시 멎고, 달려간 어머니에게 창으로 고개만 내민 운전사가 무어라고 소리쳤다. 어머니는 되돌아오고 트럭은 다시 떠났다. 우리는 어리둥절해서 서로의 얼굴을 마주 보았다. 난간을 높이 세운 짐칸에 검은 윤곽으로 우뚝우뚝 서 있던 것은 소였다. 날카롭게 구부러진 뿔들과 어둠 속에서 흐르듯

from the country village where we had taken refuge during the recent war.

"If your father could only get a job," Mother used to mutter in between spraying her tidy stacks of tobacco leaves with mouthfuls of water. She would leave at dawn, a sack chock-full of those leaves strapped to her back, and return home looking half dead two or three days later.

"I don't give up easily, but I've had it with this damn tobacco monopoly. Unless you have a license, you're always getting searched by the police. If your father could only get a job..."

Actually Father did have a job—looking up friends and classmates from the North who had immigrated to the South and somehow managed to survive the war. Finally he got a real job, selling kerosene in the city.

The day the moving truck was to come, we ate breakfast at daybreak and then camped beside the road with our bundled quilts and our household goods lashed together with cords. Lunchtime came and the truck hadn't arrived. The endlessly repeated farewells with the neighbors were over.

Toward sundown, while we were plumped listlessly on the ground, fed up with playing hopscotch

눅눅하게 들려오던 되새김질 소리도 역력했다.

소를 내려놓고 올 거예요, 짐을 부려 놓고 빈 차로 올라가는 걸 이용하면 운임이 절반이니까 아범이 그렇게 한 거예요.

어머니의 설명에, 아버지와 어머니에게 한번도 이의를 나타내 본 적이 없는 할머니는 뜨악한 표정으로, 그러나 어련히들 잘 알아서 하겠느냐는 듯 몇 번이고 고개를 주억거렸다.

그러나 트럭이 정작 우리 앞에 다시 나타난 것은 두어 시간턱이나 지난 후였다. 삼십 리 떨어진 시의 도살장에 소들을 부려 놓고 차 바닥의 오물을 닦아 내느라고 늦었다는 것이었다.

이삿짐을 다 싣고 마지막으로 어머니가 젖먹이를 안고 운전석의, 운전사와 조수의 틈에 끼어 앉자 트럭은 출발했다. 멀리 남행열차의 기적 소리가 들리는 것으로 보아 자정 무렵이었다.

나는 이삿짐들 틈에서 고개만 내밀어 깜깜하게 묻힌, 점점 멀어져 가는 마을을 보았다. 마을과 마을 뒤의 야산과 야산의 잡목숲은 한데 뭉뚱그려져 더 짙은 어둠으로 손바닥만 하게 너울대다가 마침내 하나의 점으로 털털대

and land baron, Mother took us to one of the local noodle shops and bought us each a bowl of noodle soup. The two oldest boys and I had changed into clean clothes before going outside that morning, but by now our runny noses had left a shiny track down our sleeves and on the backs of our hands.

It was dark now but Mother remained perched on the bundled quilts with our baby brother in her arms, glaring toward the approach to the bridge. Finally a pair of headlights appeared. "It's here!" Mother shouted, and we children bounced up from where we'd been sitting on the bundles. The truck stopped, but only long enough for Mother to rush over to where the driver's assistant was sticking his head out the passenger-side window. He shouted something to her over the roar of the engine and the truck pulled away. My brothers and sisters and I looked at one another in bewilderment. Those dark outlines towering above the high railing around the back of the truck were cattle. We could tell from the sharp, curved horns and the soft, liquid sound the animals made as they chewed their cud.

"They'll be back after they unload the cattle," Mother explained to Grandmother. "He arranged it that way because we pay half price if it's on its way

며 트럭의 꽁무니를 따라왔다.

읍을 벗어나자 산길이었다. 길이 바쁜 데다 서둘러 험하게 몰아대는 통에 차는 길길이 뛰고 짐들 틈바구니에 서캐처럼 박혀 있던 우리는 스프링 장치가 된 자동 인형처럼 간단없이 튀어올랐다.

할머니는 아그그그 뼈마디 부딪치는 소리를 어금니로 눌렀다. 길 아래는 강이었다. 차가 튀어오를 때마다 하마하마 강물로 곤두박질치겠지 생각하며 나는 눈을 꼭 감고 네 살짜리 동생을 힘주어 끌어안았다.

봄이라고는 해도 밤바람은 칼끝처럼 매웠다. 물살을 가르며 사납게 웅웅대던 바람은 그 첨예한 소톱으로 비듬이 허옇게 이는 살갗을 후비고 아직도 차 안에 질척하게 고여 있는 쇠똥 냄새를 한소끔씩 걷어내었다.

아까 그 소들, 다 죽었을까.

나는 문득 어둠 속에서 들려오던 소들의 눅눅한 되새김질 소리를 떠올리며 언니에게 물었다. 언니는 세운 무릎 사이에 얼굴을 깊이 묻은 채 대답이 없었다. 물론 지금쯤이면 각을 뜨고 가죽을 벗기고 내장을 훑어 내기에 충분한 시간일 것이다.

달은 줄곧 머리 위에서 둥글었고 네 살짜리 동생은 어

back to the garage without a load."

Grandmother nodded with a reluctant expression that seemed to say, "I suppose you two know what you're doing." We had never seen her disagree with Mother and Father.

A good two hours passed before the truck reappeared. After delivering the cattle to a slaughterhouse in a city ten miles away the men had had to clean the muck from the truck bed.

Mother and the baby squeezed in between the driver and his assistant after the rest of us and our baggage had been piled in back. As the truck set into motion we heard the faraway whistle of the midnight southbound train.

I stuck my head out from the bundles and watched our village recede into the night and blend with the hill behind it and its grove of scrub trees. They undulated all together, a collective darkness blacker than the night sky but looking no larger than the palm of a hand, converging finally into a single dot that bounced up and down in counterpoint with the rear of the truck.

We crossed the township line and soon we were barreling along a bumpy hillside road. Those of us in back, stuck among the bundles like nits, kept

눌한 말씨로 씨팔눔아아, 왜 자꾸 따라오는 거여어, 소리치며 달을 향해 주먹질을 해대었다.

차는 자주 섰다. 다섯 명의 아이들이 차례로 오줌이 마려웠기 때문이었다. 짐칸과 운전석 사이의 손바닥만 한 유리를 두들기면 조수가 옆창문을 열고 고개를 내밀어 돌아보며 뭐야, 하고 소리쳤다.

오줌이 마렵대요.

조수는 손짓으로 그냥 누라는 시늉을 해 보였으나 할머니가 펄쩍 뛰었다. 마지못해 차가 멎고 조수는 아이들을 하나씩 안아 내리며 한꺼번에 다 눠 버려, 몽땅, 하고 퉁명스럽게 말했다. 우리는 길바닥에 쭈그리고 앉기가 무섭게 푸드득 몸을 떨며 오래 오줌을 누었다.

행정구역이 바뀌거나 길이 굽이도는 곳에는 반드시 초소가 있어 한 차례씩 검문을 받아야 했다. 전투복을 입은 경찰이 트럭 위로 전짓불을 휘두를 때면 담배 장사로 간이 손톱만큼밖에 안 남았다는 어머니는 공연히 창 밖으로 고개를 빼어 소리쳤다.

실컷 보시오, 암만 뒤져도 같잖은 따라지 보따리와 새끼들뿐이오.

트럭은 기름을 넣기 위해 한 차례 멎고 두 번 고장이 났

bouncing up like wind-up dolls. I guessed the truck had lost its temper because of the driver's rough handling. Grandmother was doing her best to keep from crying out as she was jounced around. With each bounce I felt certain we were going to plunge into the river below, so I squeezed my eyes shut and drew my four-year-old brother close.

Though it was spring, the nighttime wind prickled our skin like a the tip of a knife. Sweeping across the river, it raked my scaling skin with its sharp nails, at the same time ridding the truck bed of the odor of cow dung.

I thought of the soft, damp sound of the cattle ruminating in the darkness. "Do you think all those cows are dead?" I asked my big sister. But she kept her face buried between her raised knees and didn't answer. Surely they'd been slaughtered, skinned, gutted, and butchered by now.

The moon kept us company, and after a while my little brother shook his fist at it: "Stupid moon, where you goin'?"

The truck had to keep stopping to let one or another of us answer nature's call. To get the driver's attention we knocked on the tiny window between the cab and the truck bed. This brought

으며 굽이굽이 수많은 검문소를 지나쳐 강과 산과 잠든 도시를 밤새도록 달려 날이 밝을 무렵 이 도시로 진입해 들어왔다. 우리가 탄 트럭의 낡은 엔진의 요란한 소리에 비로소 거리는 푸득푸득 깨어나기 시작했다.

바다를 한 뼘만치 밀어 둔 시의 끝, 해안 동네에 다다라 우리는 짐들과 함께 트럭에서 안아 내려졌다. 밤새 따라오던 달은 빛을 잃고 서쪽 하늘에 원반처럼 납작하게 걸려 있었다. 트럭이 멎은 곳은 낡은 목조의 이층집 앞이었다. 아래층은 길가에 연해 있는 상점들처럼 몇 쪽의 유리문으로 되어 있었다. 그리고 흙먼지가 부옇게 앉은 유리에 붉은 페인트로 석유 배급소라고 씌어 있었다.

바로 앞으로 우리가 살게 될 집이었다.

나는 새삼스럽게 달려드는 차가운 공기에 이빨을 마주치며 언제나 내 몫인 네 살짜리 사내 동생을 업었다.

우리가 요란하게 가로질러 온, 그리고 트럭의 뒤꽁무니 이삿짐들 틈에서 호기심과 기대로 목을 빼어 바라본 시는 내가 피난지인 시골에서 꿈꾸어 오던 도회지와는 달랐다. 나는 밀대 끝에서 피어오르는 오색의 비눗방울, 혹은 말로만 듣던 먼 나라의 크리스마스트리처럼 우리가 가게 될 도회지를 생각하곤 했었다.

the driver's assistant's head into view from the passenger window.

"What do you want!"

"We have to go to the bathroom."

With a wave of his hand the man would tell us to go where we were, but then Grandmother would raise a fuss and the driver would reluctantly stop. The assistant would lift us down one by one and then bark at us to do our business all together. We shuddered in relief as we squatted at the side of the road. It took us a long time to empty our bladders.

Whenever the truck entered a different jurisdiction, which seemed to happen at every bend in the road, there was a checkpoint. A policeman in a military uniform would play his flashlight over the truck. Mother's tobacco peddling had left her with barely enough spunk to lean out the window and yell, "Help yourself, but all you're going to find are a few lousy bundles and some kids."

All night long the truck hurtled across hills and streams and through sleeping towns, and after stopping once for gas, breaking down twice, and going through a checkpoint at every turn in the road we finally reached the city at daybreak. The streets seemed to perk up at the roar of the truck's anti-

폭이 좁은 길을 사이에 두고 조그만 베란다가 붙은, 같은 모양의 목조 이층집들이 늘어선 거리는 초라하고 지저분했으며 새벽닭의 첫 날갯짓 같은 어수선한 활기에 차 있었다. 그것은 이른 새벽 부두로 해물을 받으러 가는 장사꾼들의 자전거 페달 소리와 항만의 끝에 있는 제분 공장의 노무자들의 발길 때문이었다. 그들은 길을 메우고 버텨 선 트럭과 함부로 부려진 이삿짐을 피해 언덕을 올라갔다.

지난밤 떠나온 시골과는 모든 것이 달랐음에도 불구하고 나는 잠시, 우리가 정말 이사를 온 것일까, 낯선 곳에 온 것일까, 이상한 혼란에 빠졌다. 그것은 공기 중에 이내처럼 짙게 서려 있는, 무척 친숙하고, 내용은 잊혀진 채 분위기만 남아 있는 꿈과도 같은 냄새 때문이었다. 무슨 냄새였던가.

석유 배급소의 유리문을 밀어붙이고 나온 아버지는 약속이 틀리다고 운전사에게 고래고래 소리를 지르고 운전사는 호기심과 어쩔 수 없는 불안으로 눈을 두릿두릿 굴리고 서 있는 우리들과 이삿짐들을 번갈아 가리키며 아버지에게 삿대질을 해댔다.

목덜미에 시퍼렇게 면도 자국을 드러낸 됫박머리에 솜이 비져 나온 노란 인조 저고리를 입은, 아홉 살배기 버짐

quated engine.

At the far end of the city we arrived in a neighborhood that seemed barely able to keep the sea at arm's length, and finally we were lifted down from the truck along with our bundles. After chasing us all night the moon had long since lost its shine and was hanging flat like a disk in the western sky. The truck had stopped in front of a well-worn, two-story wooden house. The first floor looked like a shop with its sliding glass doors that opened onto the narrow street. "Kerosene retailer" had been painted in red on the dusty glass.

This was where we would live.

I felt blast of air so fresh and cold it made my teeth chatter. I was supposed to be looking out for my little brother, so I lifted him onto my back.

Rattling through the city on the truck, we had craned our necks from among the bundles and gazed out in curiosity and expectation. What we saw was different from what I had dreamed of in our country village. There I had equated the city with the rainbow-colored soap bubbles we liked to blow from the end of a homemade straw, or else the Christmas trees we'd heard about in distant lands but had never seen.

투성이 계집애인 나는 동생을 업고 이상하게 안절부절못하는 심사로 우리가 살게 될 동네를 둘러보았다.

우리의 이사 소동에 동네는 비로소 잠을 깨어 사람들은 들창을 열거나 길가에 면한 출입문으로 부스스한 머리를 내밀었다. 길을 사이에 두고 각각 여남은 채씩 늘어선 같은 모양의 목조 이층집들은 우리 집을 마지막으로 갑자기 끝났다. 그리고 우리 집에서부터 완만한 경사로 이루어진 언덕이 시작되었는데 그 언덕에는 바랜 잉크 빛깔이나 흰색 페인트로 벽을 칠한 커다란 이층집들이 길을 사이에 두고 나란히 마주 보고 서 있었다.

우리 집 앞을 지나는 길은 언덕으로 이어져 있고 언덕이 시작되는 첫째 집은 거의 우리 집과 이웃해 있었다. 그러나 넓은 벽에 비해 지나치게 작은, 창문이나 출입문이라고 볼 수 있는 문들은 모두 나무 덧문이 완강하게 닫혀져 있어 필시 빈집이거나 창고이리라는 느낌이 짙었다.

큰 덩지에 비해 지붕의 물매가 싸고 용마루가 밭아서 이상하게 눈에 설고 불균형해 뵈는 양식의 집들이었다. 그 집들은 일종의 적의로 냉담하고 무관심하게 언덕 아래를 내려다보며 서 있었다. 언덕을 넘어 선창으로 향하는 사람들의 발길에도 불구하고 언덕은 섬처럼 멀리 외따로

Our street was flanked by identical two-story frame houses with tiny balconies. It was a shabby, filthy street but the squeaky wheels of the bicycles the seafood vendors used to get to the wharf and the people tramping to work at the flour mill filled it with a chaotic energy like when chickens flap their wings at dawn. The vendors and mill workers squeezed past the truck, which had planted itself in the middle of the street, and avoiding our carelessly discharged bundles they headed up the gentle slope that began at our house.

I was lost in confusion. Everything was so different from the country village we had just left. But had we really moved? Was this really our new home? It had a dreamlike smell that filled the sky like an evening haze. It was like a once-familiar dream now forgotten, only its sensation remaining. What was that smell?

Father shoved open the door of the kerosene shop, then barked at the driver that he hadn't followed the terms of the agreement. The driver shook his fist at Father and pointed back and forth at the rest of us and our belongings. Curious and apprehensive, we could only gape at them.

There I was, a little nine-year-old with flaking

있었으며 갑각류의 동물처럼 입을 다문 집들은 초라하게, 그러나 대개의 오래된 건물이 그러하듯 역사와 남겨지지 않은 기록의 추측으로, 상상의 여백으로 다소 비장하게 바다를 향해 서 있었다.

이삿짐을 다 부려 놓고도 트럭은 시동만 걸어 놓은 채 떠나지 않았다. 요구한 액수대로 운임을 받지 못한 운전사는 지구전에 들어간 듯 운전대에 두 팔을 얹고 잠깐 눈을 붙였다.

아이 시끄러워. 또 난리가 쳐들어오나, 새벽부터 웬 지랄들이야.

젊은 여자의, 거두절미한 쇳소리가, 시위하듯 부릉대는 차 소리를 단번에 눌러 끄며 우리의 머리 위로 쨍하니 날아왔다. 어머니는, 그리고 우리는 망연해서 고개를 쳐들었다. 허벅지까지 맨살을 드러낸 채 겨우 군복 윗도리만을 어깨에 걸친 젊은 여자가 염색한 머리털을 등뒤로 너울대며 맞은편 집 이 층 베란다에서 마악 들어가려던 참이었다.

아버지는 차 바퀴 사이를 들락거리며 뺑뺑이를 치는 오빠의 덜미를 잡아 끌어내어 알밤을 먹였다. 그리고는 오르르 몰려선 우리들을 보며 일개 소대 병력이로구나 하며

skin. Beneath my gourd-bowl haircut and above the collar of my yellow synthetic jacket that was losing its batting you could have seen the bluish marks where the razor had scraped my neck. With my brother riding on my back, I looked around our new neighborhood with a strangely uneasy feeling.

The neighborhood had awakened at our noisy arrival. Heads with rumpled hair began poking out through windows and doors.

The dozen or so frame dwellings that lined the street ended abruptly with our building. The houses facing each other on the hill above also had two stories but were much larger. Some were white, others were blue-gray like faded ink.

The houses on the hill were spaced apart, except for the first one, which was enclosed by a broad wall that practically touched our house. Its door and all the windows I could see were too small and tightly shuttered. I wondered if it was actually a warehouse—no one could have lived there.

Those Western-style houses were strange, their steeply slanting roofs and pinched ridgelines looking out of place with their bulk. Perched on a hill that stood alone like a distant island amid the swarm of people on their way to the wharf, they

기막히다는 듯 헛웃음을 쳤다.

새벽 구름이 걷힌 햇살이 조금씩 투명해지기 시작할 무렵에도 언덕 위 집들은 굳게 문을 닫은 채 잠에서 깨어나지 않았다. 시의 곳곳에서 밀려난 새벽의 푸르스름한 어두움은 비를 품은 구름처럼 불길하게 언덕 위의 하늘에 몰려 있었다.

어둠이 완전히 걷히자 밤의 섬세한 발 틈으로 세류가 되어 흐르던 냄새는 억지로 참았던 긴 숨처럼 거리 곳곳에서 피어오르기 시작했다.

아, 그제야 나는 그 냄새의 정체를 알 수 있었다. 그 냄새는 낯선 감정을 대번에 지우고 거리는 친숙하고 구체적으로 내게 다가왔다. 그것은 나른한 행복감이었고 전날 떠나온 피난지의 마을에 깔먹여진 색채였으며 유년의 기억이었다.

민들레꽃이 필 무렵이 되면 나는 늘 어지럼증과 구역질로, 툇돌에 앉아 부걱부걱 거품이 이는 침을 뱉고 동생은 마당을 기어다니며 흙을 집어먹었다. 할머니는 긴 봄 내내 해인초를 끓였다. 싫어 싫어 도리질을 해대며 간신히 한 사발을 마시고 나면 나는 어쩔 수 없이 천지가 노오래지는 경험과 함께 춘곤과도 같은 이해할 수 없는 나른한

radiated an air of cool contempt. Facing out to sea, their orifices closed tight like shells, they seemed somehow heroic even in their shabbiness. How old were they? What history did they contain?

The truck started up but didn't leave. The driver hadn't been paid to his satisfaction. He rested his arms on the steering wheel and shut his eyes as if preparing for a protracted battle.

"What's all this damn commotion so early in the morning? Are the Northerners invading again?"

The blunt, hard voice passed overhead, ringing in my ears and silencing the menacing roar of the engine. Mother and then my brothers and sisters and I looked up to see a young woman on the balcony of the house across the street. Her legs were exposed to the thighs and an army jacket barely covered her shoulders. Her dyed hair swung back and forth as she went inside.

Father noticed my big brother scampering among the wheels of the truck. He grabbed him by the scruff, pulled him clear, and rapped him on the head. Then he took in the sight of us standing in a bunch. "Well, well, well," he chuckled half in amazement, "damned if we don't have ourselves a platoon here."

혼미 속에 빠져 할머니에게 지금이 아침인가 저녁인가를 때 없이 묻곤 했다. 할머니는 망할년, 회 동하나부다 라고 대꾸하며 호호 웃었다.

나는 잊혀진 꿈 속을 걸어가듯 노란빛의 혼미 속에 점차 빠져들며 문득 성큼 다가드는 언덕 위의 이층집들과 굳게 닫힌 덧창 중의 하나가 열리며 젊은 남자의 창백한 얼굴이 나타나는 것을 보았다.

어머니는 일곱 번째 아이를 배고 있어 나는 아침마다 학교에 가기 전 양재기를 들고 언덕 위 중국인들의 집 앞 길을 지나 부두로 갔다. 싱싱한 굴과 조개만이 어머니의 뒤집힌 속을 달래 주었기 때문이었다. 나는 알 수 없는 두려움과 호기심으로 흘끗거리며 굳게 닫힌 문들 앞을 달음박질쳤다. 언덕빼기로부터 스무 발자국 정도만 뜀박질하면 갑자기 중국인 거리는 끝나고 부두가 눈 아래로 펼쳐졌다. 내가 언덕의 내리받이에 이르러 가쁜 숨을 몰아쉬며 돌아볼 즈음이면 언덕의 초입에 있는 가게의 덧문을 여는 덜컹대는 소리가 들려왔다.

일주일에 한 번쯤 돼지고기를 반 근, 혹은 반의 반 근 사러 가는 푸줏간이었다. 어머니는 돈을 들려 보내며 매

Sunlight began to filter through the dawn clouds but still the shutters of the sleeping houses on the hill remained closed. As if collected from all over the city, a bluish gloom gathered ominously above the hill like clouds driven before a storm.

Finally the darkness was gone. The smell I'd first noticed, wafting through the delicate rattan blinds of the night, rose from everywhere in the streets like a deep breath at last exhaled. It was that smell that suddenly dispelled my confusion—the neighborhood now felt familiar and friendly. At last I understood: embodied in that smell was a languid happiness, an image colored by our refugee life in the village we had left the previous night, the memory of my childhood.

Later that year when the dandelions were blooming I was forever feeling dizzy and nauseated and had to sit on the shoe-ledge of our house, spitting foamy saliva while my little brother crawled about in the yard putting dirt in his mouth. It seemed as if Grandmother cooked Corsican weed all spring long. When she forced a bowl of the broth upon me I drank it reluctantly, shaking my head in disgust before sinking into a strange, languid stupor that felt like spring fever. The whole world was yellow, and

양 같은 주의를 잊지 않았다.

적게 주거든, 애라고 조금 주느냐고 말해라. 그리고 또 비계는 말고 살로 주세요, 해라.

푸줏간에서는 한쪽 볼에 힘껏 쥐어질린 듯 여문 밤톨만 한 혹이 달리고 그 혹부리에, 상기도 보이지 않는 손에 의해 끄들리고 있는 듯 길게 뻗친 수염을 기른 홀아비 중국인이 고기를 팔았다.

애라고 조금 주세요?

키가 작아 발돋움질로 간신히 진열대에 턱을 올려놓고 돈을 밀어넣는 것과 동시에 나는 총알처럼 내뱉었다.

고기를 자르기 위해 벽에 매단 가죽끈에 칼을 문질러 날을 세우던 중국인은 미처 무슨 말인지 몰라 뚱한 얼굴로 나를 바라보았다. 나는 비계는 말고 살로 달래라 하던 어머니의 말을 하기 전 중국인이 고기를 자를까 봐 허겁지겁 내쏘았다.

고기로 달래요.

중국인은 꾸룩꾸룩 웃으며 그때야 비로소 고기를 덥석 베어 내었다.

왜 고기만 주니, 털도 주고 가죽도 주지.

푸줏간에 잇대어 후추나 흑설탕, 근으로 달아 주는 중

regardless of the time I was always asking Grandmother whether it was morning or evening.

"Are the worms stirring, you little stinker?" she would retort with a hearty laugh.

One day while I was descending into my yellow stupor, feeling like I was walking into a forgotten dream, the two-story houses on the hill suddenly swooped close, one of the shutters opened, and the pale face of a young man appeared.

Mother was pregnant: this would be baby number seven. Fresh oysters and clams were the only foods that could soothe her queasy stomach, so every morning before school I set off over the hill for the pier, aluminum bowl in hand. I dashed by the firmly shut gates of the houses on the hill, sneaking glances at them out of curiosity and a vague anxiety, for those were the houses of the Chinese. A mere twenty steps down the other side of the hill the Chinese district abruptly ended at a butcher shop and the pier unfolded before my eyes. I would stop to catch my breath and look back, and if I had timed it right the shutters of the shop would clatter open.

I went there every week to buy half a pound of

국차 따위를 파는 잡화점이 있었다. 이 거리에 있는 단 하나의 중국인 가게였다. 우리 동네 사람들은 가끔 돼지고기를 사러 푸줏간에 갈 뿐 잡화점에는 가지 않았다. 우리에게는 옷이나 신발에 다는 장식용 구슬, 염색물감, 폭죽놀이에 쓰이는 화약 따위가 필요치 않았기 때문이었다.

햇빛이 밝은 날에도 한쪽 덧문만 열린 가게는 어둡고 먼지가 낀듯 침침했다.

그러나 저녁 무렵이 되면 바구니를 팔에 건 중국인들이 모여들었다. 뒤통수에 쇠똥처럼 바짝 말아붙인 머리를 조금씩 흔들며 엄청나게 두꺼운 귓불에 은고리를 달고 전족한 발을 뒤뚱거리며 여자들은 여러 갈래로 난 길을 통해 마치 땅거미처럼 스름스름 중국인 거리를 향했다.

남자들은 가게 앞에 내놓은 의자에 앉아 말없이 오랫동안 대통 담배를 피우다가 올 때처럼 사라졌다. 그들은 대개 늙은이들이었다.

우리는 찻길과 인도를 가름짓는 낮고 좁은 턱에 엉덩이를 붙이고 나란히 앉아 발장단을 치며 그들을 손가락질했다.

아편을 피우고 있는 거야, 더러운 아편쟁이들.

정말 긴 대통을 통해 나오는 연기는 심상치 않은 노오

pork. Mother would place money in my hand and send me on my way, always with the same warning: "If he doesn't give you enough, ask him if it's because you're a child. And ask him to give you only lean meat, not fat."

The butcher was a Chinese widower whose cheek sported a chestnut-sized growth. It looked as if someone had given him a terrific punch. Long hairs trailed from the growth, as if pulled by an unseen hand.

The first time I went there I found the man stropping his butcher knife.

"Are you only giving me this much because I'm a child?" I blurted. By standing on tiptoe I was just able to get my chin over the counter as I stuck out the money.

The man turned and looked at me, baffled.

Afraid he would cut the meat before I could finish saying what Mother had told me, I snapped, "She told me to ask for lean."

Stifling a laugh, the butcher quickly sliced the meat for me. "Why only lean? I can give you some hair and skin too."

Next to the butcher shop was a store that sold such items as pepper, brown sugar, and Chinese tea

란 빛으로 흐트러지고 있었다.

늙은 중국인들은 이러한 우리들에게 가끔 미소를 지었다.

통틀어 중국인 거리라고 불리는 동네에, 바로 그들과 인접해 살고 있으면서도 그들 중국인에게 관심을 갖는 것은 아이들뿐이었다. 어른들은 무관심하게, 그러나 경멸하는 어조로 '뙈놈들'이라고 말했다.

우리는 그들과 전혀 접촉이 없었음에도, 언덕 위의 이층집, 그 속에 사는 사람들은 한없이 상상과 호기심의 효모였다.

그들은 우리에게 밀수업자, 아편쟁이, 누더기의 바늘땀마다 금을 넣는 쿠리, 그리고 말발굽을 울리며 언 땅을 휘몰아치는 마적단, 원수의 생 간을 내어 형님도 한 점, 아우도 한 점 씹어 먹는 오랑캐, 사람 고기로 만두를 빚는 백정, 뒤를 보면 바지도 올리기 전 꽛꽛이 언 채 서 있다는 북만주 벌판의 똥덩어리였다. 굳게 닫힌 문의 안쪽에 있는 것은, 십 년을 사귀어도 좀체 내뵈지 않는다는 깊은 흉중에 든 것은 금인가, 아편인가, 의심인가.

우리 집에서 숙제하지 않을래?

집 앞에 이르러 치옥이가 이불과 담요가 널린 이 층의

in bulk. It was the only general store in Chinatown. The people from our neighborhood occasionally went to the butcher shop for pork but didn't shop at the general store. We had no use for dyes and firecrackers and we didn't need decorative beads for our clothing and shoes.

The store's shutters were opened on one side only, and even on bright, sunny days the interior was dark and gloomy, as if enveloped in dust. But in the evening the Chinese flocked there, creeping like dusk through interlocking alleys. The women had great thick ears and wore silver earrings. They tottered on bound feet, baskets over their arms, their heads bobbing and the tight buns of hair resembling mounds of cow dung.

While the women shopped the men sat in chairs in front of the store and silently smoked their long bamboo pipes before creeping back home. Most of them were elderly.

We children parked ourselves in a row on the narrow, low curb, tapping our feet on the street and pointing at the men.

"Look at those dirty addicts—they're smoking opium."

And in fact the smoke scattering from the pipes

베란다를 올려다보며 나를 끌었다. 베란다에 이불이 널린 것은 매기 언니가 집에 없다는 표시였다. 매기 언니는 집에서는 언제나 담요를 씌운 침대 속에 들어가 있었다. 나는 맞은편의 우리 집을 흘긋거리며 망설였다. 할머니나 어머니는 치옥이네를 양갈보집이라고 불렀다. 그러나 이 거리의 적산가옥들 중 양갈보에게 방을 세주지 않은 것은 우리 집뿐이었다. 그네들은 거리로 면한 문을 활짝 열어 놓고 거리낌없이 미군에게 허리를 안겼으며 볕 잘 드는 베란다에 레이스가 달린 여러 가지 빛깔의 속옷들과 때 묻은 담요를 널어 지난밤의 분방한 습기를 말렸다. 여자의 옷은, 더욱이 속엣것은 방 안에 줄을 매고야 너는 것으로 알고 있는 할머니는, 천하의 망종들이라고 고개를 돌렸다.

치옥이의 부모는 아래층을 쓰고 위층의 큰방은 매기 언니가 검둥이들과 함께 세 들어 있었다. 치옥이는 큰방을 거쳐 가야 하는 협실과도 같은 좁고 긴 방을 썼다. 때문에 나는 아침마다 치옥이를 부르러 가면 그때까지도 침대 속에 머리칼을 흩뜨리고 누워 있는 매기 언니와 화장대의 의자에 거북스럽게 몸을 구부리고 앉아 조그만 은빛 가위로 콧수염을 가다듬는 비대한 검둥이를 만났다. 매기 언

was unusually yellow.

Now and then the elderly men gave us a smile.

Our families lived right next to Chinatown but we children were the only ones who were interested in the Chinese. The grownups referred to them indifferently as "Chinks."

Although we had no direct contact with the Chinese in the two-story houses on the hill, they were the yeast of our infinite imagination and curiosity. Smugglers, opium addicts, coolies who squirreled away gold inside every panel of their ragged quilted clothing, mounted bandits who swept over the frozen earth to the beat of their horses' hoofs, barbarians who sliced up the raw liver of a slaughtered enemy and ate it according to rank, outcaste butchers who made wonton out of human flesh, people whose turds had frozen upright on the northern Manchurian plain before they could pull up their pants—this was how we thought of them. What was inside the tightly closed shutters of their houses? And what lay deep inside their minds, seldom expressed even after years of friendship? Was it gold? Opium? Suspicion?

"Let's do our homework here," Ch'i-ok said when

니는 누운 채로 손을 까닥거려 들어오라는 시늉을 했으나 나는 반쯤 열린 문가에 비켜서서 방 안을 흘끔거리며 치옥이를 기다렸다. 나는 검둥이가 우울한 남자라고 생각했다. 맥없이 늘어진 두꺼운 가슴팍의 살, 잿빛 눈, 또한 우물거리는 말투와 내게 한 번도 웃어 보인 적이 없다는 것이 그러한 느낌을 갖게 한 것이다.

학교 갈 때는 길에서 불러라. 검둥이는 네가 아침에 오는 게 싫대.

치옥이가 말했으나 나는 매일 아침 삐걱대는 층계를 밟고 올라가 매기 언니의 방문 앞을 서성이며 치옥이를 불렀다.

매기 언니는 밤에 온다고 그랬어, 침대에서 놀아도 괜찮아.

입덧이 심한 어머니는 매사가 귀찮다는 얼굴로 안방에 드러누워 있을 것이고 오빠는 땅강아지를 잡으러 갔을 것이다. 할머니는 기다렸다는 듯 막 젖이 떨어진 막내 동생을 업혀 내쫓을 것이었다.

커튼으로 햇빛을 가린 어두운 방의 침대에 매기 언니의 딸인 제니가 자고 있었다. 치옥이는 벽장 문을 열고 비스킷 상자를 꺼내어 꼭 두 개만 집어 들고는 잘 닫아 다시

we arrived at her house. She looked up toward the quilt and blanket stretched over the side of the second-floor balcony. This was a sign that Maggie was out. If she were in, she would have been in bed, beneath the blanket. I hesitated, glancing across the street at our house. Mother and Grandmother referred to Ch'i-ok's house as a whorehouse for the GIs. Our house was the only one in the neighborhood that didn't rent out a room to a prostitute. These women threw open their doors to the street and thought nothing of letting the American soldiers give them a squeeze. Stained blankets and colorful underwear festooned with lace hung on the sunny balconies, drying from the free-spirited activities of the previous night.

"Scum!" Grandmother would say, turning away from the sight. To her way of thinking, women's clothes, and especially their underwear, should be hung to dry inside.

Ch'i-ok's parents lived downstairs and Maggie rented the big room upstairs with a darky GI. Ch'i-ok had to go through Maggie's room to get to her own, which was small and narrow like a closet. When I went to get Ch'i-ok for school in the morning I always encountered Maggie lying in bed with

넣었다. 비스킷은 달고, 연한 치약 냄새가 났다.

이거 참 예쁘다.

내가 화장대의 향수병을 가리키자 치옥이는 그것을 거꾸로 들고 솔솔 겨드랑이에 뿌리는 시늉을 하며 미제야, 라고 말했다. 치옥이는 다시 벽장 속에 손을 넣어 부스럭대더니 사탕을 두 알 꺼냈다.

이거 참 맛있다.

응, 미제니까.

치옥이가 또 새침하게 대답했다. 제니가 눈을 말갛게 뜨고 우리를 보고 있었다.

제니, 예쁘지? 언니들은 숙제를 해야 하니까 조금만 더 자렴.

치옥이가 부드럽게 말하며 손바닥으로 눈꺼풀을 쓸어 덮자 제니는 깜빡이 인형처럼 눈을 꼭 감았다.

매기 언니의 방에서는 무엇이든 신기했다. 치옥이는 내가 매양 탄성으로 어루만지는 유리병, 화장품, 페티코트, 속눈썹 따위를 조금씩만 만지게 하고는 이내 손댄 흔적이 없이 본디대로 해 놓았다.

좋은 수가 있어.

치옥이 침대 머릿장에서 초록색의 액체가 반쯤 남겨진

her hair disheveled and the huge darky sitting hunched in front of the dresser trimming his mustache with a tiny pair of silvery scissors. Maggie would beckon me in with the slightest motion of her hand but I always remained outside the half-open door, peeking inside while I waited for Ch'i-ok. The thick flesh of the darky's chest looked like molded rubber and his eyes were smoky. He always mumbled when he spoke, and he never smiled at me. What a gloomy man, I thought.

"Can't you call me from the street?" Ch'i-ok once asked. "The darky doesn't like you going up there."

But every morning I walked up the creaky stairs and called to Ch'i-ok while hovering outside Maggie's room.

"Maggie said she won't be back until tonight. We can play on her bed," Ch'i-ok cajoled me.

I thought for a moment: Mother had a bad case of morning sickness and was probably lying in the family room, looking vexed at everything. My older brother had likely gone outside to catch mole crickets. And I knew that as soon as I walked in, Grandmother would tell me to piggyback my baby brother, who had just been weaned, and then shoo me out of the house.

표주박 모양의 병을 꺼냈다. 병의 초록색이 찰랑대는 부분에 손톱을 대어 금을 만든 뒤 뚜껑을 열어 그것을 따라 내게 내밀었다.

먹어 봐. 달고 화하단다.

내가 한 모금에 홀짝 마시자 치옥이는 다시 뚜껑을 가득 채워 꿀꺽 마셨다. 그리고 손톱을 대고 있던 금부터 손가락 두 마디만큼 초록색 술이 줄어들자 줄어든 만큼 냉수를 부어 뚜껑을 닫아 머릿장에 넣었다.

감쪽같잖니? 어떻니? 맛있지?

입안은 박하를 한 입 문 듯 상쾌하게 화끈거렸다.

이건 비밀이야.

매기 언니의 방에서는 무엇이든 비밀이었다. 서랍장의 옷갈피짬에서 꺼낸 비로드 상자 속에는 세 줄짜리 진주목걸이, 여러 가지 빛깔로 야단스럽게 물들인 유리알 브로치, 귀걸이 따위가 들어 있었다. 치옥이는 그중 알이 굵은 유리 목걸이를 걸고 거울 앞에서 단호하게 말했다.

난 커서 양갈보가 될 테야, 매기 언니가 목걸이도 구두도 옷도 다 준댔어.

손끝도 발끝도 저리듯 나른히 맥이 풀려 왔다. 눈꺼풀이 무겁고 숨이 차오는 건 방 안이 너무 어둡기 때문일까,

And so I followed Ch'i-ok upstairs. Jennie, Maggie's daughter, was asleep on the bed. Curtains kept the sun out and the room dim.

Ch'i-ok opened the storage cabinet, located a box of cookies, took two of them, and carefully replaced the box. The cookies were sweet and smelled faintly like toothpaste.

"That's so pretty," I said, pointing to a bottle of perfume on the dresser.

Ch'i-ok turned it upside down and pretended to gently spray her armpits. "Made in America." Again she reached inside the cabinet and rustled around, this time producing two candies.

"It tastes so good," I said.

"Mmm, because it's made in America," Ch'i-ok answered in the same blase tone.

Jennie was now wide awake and watching us.

"Jennie, aren't you pretty? Now we have to do our homework, so why don't you go back to sleep for a little while?" Ch'i-ok spoke softly, brushing Jennie's eyelids down with her palm, and in an instant the little girl's eyes had closed tightly like those of a doll.

Everything in Maggie's room was marvelous. Ch'i-ok let me feel each of the belongings just for a moment, and every one of them brought a joyful

숨을 내쉴 때마다 박하 냄새가 하얗게 뿜어져 나왔다. 나는 베란다로 통한 유리문의 커튼을 열었다. 노오란 햇빛이 다글다글 끓으며 들어와 먼지를 떠올려 방 안은 온실과도 같았다. 나는 문의 쇠 장식에 달아오른 뺨을 대며 바깥을 내다보았다. 그리고 다시 중국인 거리의 이층집 열린 덧문과 이켠을 보고 있는 젊은 남자의 얼굴을 보았다. 그러자 알지 못할 슬픔이, 비애라고나 말해야 할 아픔이 가슴에서부터 파상을 이루며 전신으로 퍼져 나갔다.

왜 그러니? 어지럽니?

이미 초록색 물의 성질을, 그 효과를 알고 있는 치옥이 다가와 나란히 문에 매달렸다. 나는 고개를 저었다. 그럴 수밖에 없는 것이 나는 이층집 창문에서 비롯되는 감정을 알 수도, 설명할 수도 없었으며 그 순간 나무 덧문이 무겁게 닫혀지고 남자의 모습이 사라졌기 때문이었다.

유리 목걸이에 햇빛이 갖가지 빛깔로 쟁강쟁강 튀었다. 그중 한 알을 입술에 물며 치옥이가 말했다.

난 양갈보가 될 거야.

나는 커튼을 닫고 돌아와 침대에 누웠다. 그는 누구일까. 나는 기억나지 않는 꿈을 되살려 보려는 안타까움에 잠겨 생각했다. 지난 가을에도 나는 그를 보았다. 이발소

exclamation from me as I caressed it. Then we replaced each item, leaving no sign that we'd tampered with it.

"I have an idea."

Ch'i-ok reached inside a cabinet at the head of the bed and took out a gourd-shaped bottle half full of a green liquid. After making a line with her fingernail on the side of the bottle to mark the level of the liquid she opened the bottle, poured a small amount into the cap, and handed it to me.

"Try it. It's sweet—tastes like menthol."

I quickly drank it and returned the cap to Ch'i-ok. She filled it for herself and gulped it. That brought the level of the liquid about two fingers below the mark. Ch'i-ok made up the difference with water, capped the bottle, and returned it to the cabinet.

"Perfect! How was it—tasty, huh?"

The inside of my mouth was nice and warm, as if I had a mouthful of peppermint.

"Now don't tell anyone," Ch'i-ok said as she removed a velvet box from among some clothes in one of the dresser drawers.

Everything in Maggie's room was a secret.

The box contained a pearl necklace long enough to make three strands, a brooch adorned with gar-

에서였다. 키가 작아 의자에 널빤지를 얹고 앉아 나는 어머니가 일러준 대로 말했다.

상고머리예요. 가뜩이나 밉상인데 됫박머리는 안 돼요.

그런데 다 깎은 뒤 거울 속에 남은 것은 여전히 됫박머리였다.

이왕 깎은 걸 어떡하니 다음 번에 다시 잘 깎아 주마.

그러기에 왜 아저씨는 이발만 열심히 하지 잡담을 하느냔 말예요.

나는 바락바락 악을 썼다. 마침내 이발사는 덜컥 의자를 젖히며 말했다.

정말 접시처럼 발랑 되바라진 애구나, 못 쓰겠어. 엄마 뱃속에서 나올 때 주둥이부터 나왔니?

못 쓰면 끈달아 쓸 테니 걱정 말아요. 아저씨는 손모가지에 가위부터 들고 나와 이발쟁이가 됐단 말예요?

이발소 안이 와아 웃음바다가 되었다. 나는 의기양양해서 사람들을 둘러보았다. 웃지 않는 건 이발사와 구석자리의 의자에 턱수건을 두르고 앉은 젊은 남자뿐이었다. 그는 거울 속에서 물끄러미 나를 보고 있었다. 나는 문득 그가 중국인 남자라고 생각했다. 길 건너 비스듬히 엇비낀 거리에서만 보았을 뿐 한 번도 가까이서 본 적이 없었

ishly colored glass beads, some earrings, and other jewelry. Ch'i-ok tried on a necklace made of thick glass beads and studied herself in the mirror.

"I'm going to be a GI's whore when I grow up," she said decisively. "Maggie said she'll give me necklaces, shoes, things to wear—everything."

I felt like the tips of my fingers and toes had gone to sleep and I was dissolving. I was short of breath and couldn't keep my eyes open. Was it the darkness of the room? I imagined the peppermint leaving a white trail every time I breathed out. I drew aside the curtain covering the door to the balcony and seething yellow sunlight came in, illuminating the dust and making the room look like a greenhouse. I touched my burning cheek to the the doorknob and peered outside. Once again I saw the two-story house in Chinatown with the open shutter and the face of the young man looking my way. A mysterious sadness, an ineffable pathos began undulating in my chest and then it spread through me.

"What's the matter? Are you dizzy?" asked Ch'i-ok, who knew what the green liquid was and how it affected you. She snuggled up beside me against the door to the balcony.

으나 그 알 수 없는 시선의 느낌이 그러했다. 나는 목수건을 풀어 탁 거울 앞에 던져 놓았다. 그리고 또각또각 걸어 나가 두 손으로 허리를 짚고 문께에 서서 말했다.

죽을 때까지 이발쟁이나 해요.

그러고는 달음질쳐 집으로 돌아왔다. 아버지는 피난 시절의 셋방살이, 혹은 다리 밑이나 천막에서 아이들을 끌어안고 밤을 새우던 기억에 복수라도 하듯 끊임없이 집 손질을 했다. 손바닥만 한 마당을 없애며, 바느질을 처음 배운 계집애들이 가방의 안쪽이나 옷의 갈피짬마다 비밀 주머니를 만들어 붙이듯 방을 들이고 마루를 깔았다. 때문에 집 안에는 개미굴같이 복잡하게 얽힌 좁고 긴 통로가 느닷없이 나타나고, 숨으면 아무도 찾아낼 수 없는 장소가 꼭 한 군데는 있기 마련이었다.

나는 집으로 뛰어 들어와 헌 옷가지나 묵은 살림살이 따위 잡동사니가 들어찬 변소 옆의 골방에 숨어들어 갔다. 빈 항아리의 좁은 아구리에 얼굴을 들이밀어도 온몸의 뼈가 물러앉는 듯한 센 물살과도 같은 슬픔은 사라지지 않았다.

그 뒤로도 나는 여러 차례 창을 열고 이켠을 보고 있는 그 남자의 시선을 느낄 수 있었다. 대개 배급소의 문 밖에

I shook my head, unable to understand, much less explain the feeling I had in response to the face in the second-floor window, and the next moment the wooden shutter thumped shut and the young man disappeared from view.

The glass beads of Ch'i-ok's necklace clicked together, their colors dancing in the sunlight. Ch'i-ok took one of the beads in her lips. "I'm going to be a GI's whore."

I drew the curtain and lay down on the bed. Who could he be? I tried fretfully to revive my memories of a forgotten dream. I knew I'd seen him the previous autumn at the barber's. I'd had to sit on a plank placed across the chair because I was so short. I had instructed the barber as Mother had told me:

"Please make it short and layered on the sides and back but leave it long on top. I'm ugly enough already, so a gourd-bowl haircut is no good."

But when I looked in the mirror after the barber finished, I still had a gourd bowl.

"Too late to complain. But I'll do better next time—promise."

"I knew this would happen! Why can't you concentrate on cutting hair instead of gabbing with everybody?"

쭈그리고 앉아 석간신문을 기다리고 있을 때였다.

제니, 제니, 일어나. 엄마가 왔다.

치옥이가 꾸며 낸, 부드럽고 달콤한 목소리로 제니를 부르자 제니가 눈을 뜨고 일어나 앉았다. 치옥이가 아래층에서 대야에 물을 떠 왔다. 제니는 비눗물이 눈에 들어가도 울지 않았다. 우리는 제니의 머리를 빗기고 향수를 뿌리고 옷장을 뒤져 옷을 갈아입혔다. 백인 혼혈아인 제니는 다섯 살이 되었어도 말을 못했다. 혼자 옷을 입는 것은 물론 숟갈질도 못해 밥을 떠 넣어 주면 한 귀로 주르르 흘렸다. 검둥이가 있을 때면 제니는 늘 치옥이의 방에 있었다.

짐승의 새끼야.

할머니는 어쩌다 문 밖이나 베란다에 있는 제니를 보고 신기하다는 듯 혹은 할머니가 제일 싫어하는, 털 가진 짐승을 볼 때의 혐오의 눈으로 보며 말했다. 나는 제니를 보는 할머니의 눈초리가 무서웠다. 언젠가 집에 쥐가 끓어 고양이를 한 마리 기른 적이 있었다. 고양이가 골방에서 새끼를 일곱 마리나 낳자 할머니는 고양이에게 미역국을 갖다 주었다. 그리고는 똑바로 고양이의 눈을 쳐다보며 나비가 쥐 새끼를 낳았구나, 쥐 새끼를 일곱 마리나 낳았

The barber jerked the plank away from under me. "What a smart-alecky little girl. That's no way to talk. I'll bet that yap of yours was the first thing that came out when you were born."

"Don't you worry about how I should talk. And I'll bet you're a hair chopper because you came out with scissors around your wrist."

The other customers roared with laughter. I looked around with a triumphant air. The only ones who weren't laughing were the barber and a young man sitting in the corner with a bib around his neck. The young man was studying me in the mirror. *He's Chinese*, I suddenly thought. Although I had seen him only at an angle from across the street, never close up, his inscrutable gaze had given me that impression. I took the towel from around my neck and tossed it in front of the mirror. Then I stamped to the doorway, put my hands on my hips, and turned back: "Until the day you die you'll be nothing but a hair chopper!" And then I ran home.

Father was constantly remodeling our house, as if to compensate for the privations of our refugee life in the country village—the entire family crowded into a single rented room, and before that the many

구나 하고 노래의 후렴처럼 몇 번이고 되풀이했다. 그날 밤 고양이는 새끼를 모조리 잡아먹고 대가리만 남겨 피칠한 입으로 야옹야옹 밤새 울었다. 할머니는 기다렸다는 듯 일곱 개의 조그만 대가리들을 신문지에 싸서 하수구에 버렸다. 할머니가 유난히 정갈하고 성품이 차가운 것은 한 번도 자식을 실어 보지 못했기 때문이라고 어머니는 말하곤 했다. 할머니는 어머니의 서모였다. 시집온 지 석 달 만에 영감님이 처제를 봤다지 뭐예요. 글쎄, 그래서 평생 조면하시고 의붓딸에게 의탁하신 거지요. 어머니는 먼 친척 할머니에게 소리를 낮춰 수군거렸다.

제니는 치옥이의 살아 있는 인형이었다. 목욕을 시켜도, 삼십 분마다 한 번씩 옷을 갈아입혀도 매기 언니는 나무라지 않았다. 제니는 아기가 되고 때로 환자가 되고 때로 천사도 되었다. 나는 진심으로 치옥이가 부러웠다.

너도 동생이 있잖아.

치옥이가 의아하게 물었다.

의붓동생인걸.

그럼 늬네 친엄마가 아니니?

나는 마른침을 꿀꺽 삼켰다.

응, 계모야.

sleepless nights he had spent keeping the children warm in his arms under a bridge or inside a tent. He got rid of our tiny yard, adding a room and a veranda to the house in the way that girls who have just learned how to sew might add secret pockets to the inside of a book bag or the underside of their clothing. And so a mazelike hallway appeared inside, long and narrow like an ant tunnel.

Along with the hallway there materialized a place where I could hide and no one would find me—the back room next to the toilet, where we kept old clothing, household stuff, and various odds and ends. The day of the ill-fated haircut I ran home, sneaked into that room, and pressed my face against the narrow mouth of a jar hoping in vain that the sorrow sweeping over my bones like a strong current would empty into it.

Several times after that, usually when I was hunkered down in front of Father's shop waiting for the evening newspaper, I sensed that the young Chinese man had opened his window and was looking toward me.

"Jennie. Time to get up, Jennie—your mom's here," Ch'i-ok said in an affectedly sweet and gentle tone. Jennie opened her eyes and sat up. Ch'i-ok

그렇구나, 어쩐지 그럴 거라고 생각했었어. 이건 비밀인데 우리 엄마도 계모야.

치옥이는 비밀이라고 했지만 치옥이가 의붓자식이라는 것을 모르는 사람은 동네에서 아무도 없었다. 우리는 비밀을 서로 지켜 주기로 손가락을 걸고 맹세했다.

그럼 너의 엄마도 널 때리고, 나가 죽으라고 하니?

응, 아무도 없을 때면.

치옥이는 바지를 내려 허벅지의 피멍을 보이며 단호하게 말했다.

난 나가서 양갈보가 되겠어.

나는 얼마나 자주 정말 내가 의붓자식이었기를, 그래서 맘대로 나가 버릴 수 있기를 바랐는지 몰랐다.

어머니는 일곱 번째 아이를 배고 있었다. 가난한 중국인 거리에 사는 우리들 중 아기는 한밤중 천사가 안고 오는 것이라든지 방긋 웃으며 배꼽으로 나오는 것이라는 것을 믿는 아이는 아무도 없었다. 여자의 벌거벗은 두 다리 짬에서 비명을 지르며 나온다는 것쯤은 누구나 알고 있었다.

러닝셔츠 바람의 지아이들이 부대 안의 테니스 코트에 모여 칼 던지기를 하고 있었다. 동심원이 그려진 과녁을

fetched a basin of water from downstairs. Jennie didn't cry even when the soapy water got in her eyes. We combed her hair, sprayed her with perfume, and changed her into clothes from the closet. Jennie's father was white and her mother Korean and at the age of five she still hadn't begun to talk. She couldn't feed herself, much less put on her own clothes, and what she was fed tended to trickle out the side of her mouth. When the darky was there Jennie had to be moved to Ch'i-ok's room.

Grandmother occasionally noticed Jennie on the balcony or outside the house. "Whelp!" she would say, looking at the girl almost in amazement, her eyes filled with the hatred she reserved for fur-bearing animals. She frightened me when she stared at Jennie like that. Some time ago, after our house was infested with rats, we had gotten a cat. The cat bore a litter of seven kittens in the back room. Grandmother fed it seaweed soup to help it recover, then stared right into the cat's eyes and repeated like a refrain, "Kitty had some baby rats, seven baby rats." That evening the cat ate all seven kittens, leaving only the heads. Then it yowled all night long, not bothering to clean its bloodstained mouth. As if she'd expected this, Grandmother wrapped the

향해 칼은 은빛 침처럼, 빛의 한 순간처럼, 청년의 머리에 돋아난 새치처럼 날카롭게 빛나며 공기를 갈랐다.

휙휙 바람을 일으키며 휘파람처럼 날아드는 칼이 동심원 안의 검은 점에 정확히 꽂힐 때마다 그들은 우우 짐승 같은 함성을 질렀고 우리는 뜨거운 침을 삼키며 아아 목젖을 떨었다.

목표를 정확히 맞히고 한 걸음씩 물러나 목표물과의 거리를 넓히며 칼을 던지던 백인 지아이가, 칼이 손 안에서 튕겨져 나오려는 순간 갑자기 발의 방향을 바꾸었다. 칼은 바람을 찢는 날카로운 소리로 우리를 향해 날았다. 우리는 아악 비명을 지르며 철조망 아래로 납작 엎드렸다. 다리 사이가 뜨뜻하게 젖어 왔다. 그리고 잠시 후 고개를 들어 킬킬대는 미군의 손짓이 가리키는 곳을 하얗게 질린 얼굴로 바라보았다. 우리의 뒤 두어 걸음쯤 떨어진 곳에서 가슴에 칼을 맞은 고양이가 네 발을 허공에 쳐들고 반듯이 누워 있었다. 거의 작은 개만큼이나 큰 검정 고양이였다. 부대의 쓰레기통을 뒤지는 도둑고양이였을 것이다. 우리가 다가가 둘러섰을 때까지도 날카로운 수염발이 바르르 떨리고 있었다. 갑자기 오빠가 고양이를 집어올렸다. 그리고 뛰었다. 우리도 뒤를 따라 덩달아 뛰기 시작했

seven tiny heads in newspaper and sent them down the sewer drain.

Mother used to tell me that the reason Grandmother was so heartless and cold was that she'd never had children of her own. She was actually a kind of stepmother to Mother. I had once overheard Mother whispering about Grandmother to an elderly woman who was a distant relative: "They were married only three months when that father of mine had an affair with her sister—can you believe it? That's why they separated and she eventually decided to come live with us."

Jennie was like a doll to Ch'i-ok. Ch'i-ok could give her a bath and change her clothes every half hour and never get a scolding from Maggie. To Ch'i-ok Jennie was sometimes a baby, sometimes a sick little girl, sometimes an angel. I envied Ch'i-ok with all my heart and it must have shown on my face.

"Don't you have a sister too?" Ch'i-ok asked me dubiously.

"She's my stepsister."

"You mean that's not your real mother?"

"My stepmother," I lied with a lump in my throat.

Tears gathered in her eyes. "Well. Somehow I had a hunch. Don't tell anyone but I have a stepmother

다. 젖은 속옷이 살에 감겨 쓰라렸다.

미군 부대의 막사가 보이지 않는 곳에 이르자 오빠가 헉헉대며 걸음을 멈추었다. 그리고 비로소 손에 들린 것이 무엇인지 깨달은 듯 진저리를 치며 내동댕이쳤다. 검은 고양이는 털썩 둔탁한 소리를 내며 땅바닥에 떨어졌다.

그걸 왜 갖고 왔니?

한 아이가 비난하는 어조로 말했다. 도전을 받은 꼬마 나폴레옹은 분연히 고양이의 가슴팍에 꽂힌, 끝이 송곳처럼 가늘고 날카로운 칼을 빼어 풀섶에 쓱쓱 피를 닦았다. 그리고 찰칵 날을 숨겨 주머니에 넣었다.

막대기를 가져와.

한 아이가 지난 봄 식목일의 기념식수 가지를 잘라 왔다.

오빠는 혁대를 끌러 고양이의 목에 감고 그 끝을 나뭇가지에 매었다. 그리고 우리는 묵묵히 거리를 지났다.

고양이는 한없이 늘어져 발이 땅에 끌리고 그 무게로 오빠의 어깨에 얹힌 나뭇가지는 활처럼 휘었다.

중국인 거리에 다다랐을 때 여름의 긴긴 해는 한없이 긴 고양이의 허리를 자르며 비껴 기울고 있었다.

머리에 서릿발이 얹힌 듯 희끗희끗 밀가루를 뒤집어쓴 제분 공장 노무자들이 빈 도시락을 달그락거리며 언덕을

too."

There wasn't a soul in our neighborhood who didn't know this.

I linked my little finger with Ch'i-ok's and we promised to keep each other's secret.

"Does your mom beat you and tell you to get lost and drop dead?" I asked.

"Yeah, when no one's around." Ch'i-ok lowered her pants and showed me her bruised thighs. "I'm going to run away and be a GI's whore."

How often I wished I really were a stepdaughter so I could run away whenever I pleased.

Mother was still carrying baby number seven. None of us children in this poor district next to Chinatown believed that babies were brought to earth in the arms of an angel in the middle of the night. And they didn't emerge with bright smiles from their mother's belly button. Everyone knew a baby came out screaming from between the naked legs of a woman.

GIs in T-shirts were doing target practice with knives on one of the tennis courts at the army base. The knives cut through the air like silver needles toward the concentric circles on the target, giving

넘어 우리 곁을 지나쳐 갔다.

고양이의 검고 긴 몸뚱아리, 우리들의 끝없이 길고 두려운 저녁 무렵의 그림자를 밟으며 우리는 부두를 향해 걸었다. 그때 나는 다시 보았다. 이 층의 덧문을 열고 그는 슬픈 듯, 노여운 듯 어쩌면 희미하게 웃는 듯한 알 수 없는 눈길로 우리의 행렬을 보고 있었다.

부두에 이르러 우리는 나뭇가지를 내려놓고 고양이의 목에서 혁대를 풀었다. 오빠는 침을 퉤퉤 뱉으며 자꾸 흘러내리려는 허리를 혁대로 단단히 죄었다.

그리고 쓰레기와 빈 병과 배를 허옇게 뒤집고 떠 있는 썩은 생선들이 떠밀려 범람하는 방죽 아래로 고양이를 떨어뜨렸다.

해가 지고 있었으므로 우리는 공원으로 가기로 했다.

여느 때 같으면 한없이 올라가는 공원의 층계에 엎드려 층계를 올라가는 양갈보들의 치마 밑을 들여다보며, 고래힘줄로 심을 넣어 바구니처럼 둥글게 부풀린 패티코트 속이 온통 맨다리뿐이라는 데 탄성을 지르거나 혹은 풀섶에 질펀히 앉아서 '도라아 보는 발거름마다 눈무울 젖은 내애 처엉춘, 한마아는 과거사를 도리켜 보올때에 아아 산타마리아아의 종이이 우울리인다' 따위 늙은 창부 타령을 찢

off a piercing glint, a flash of light, a brightness like a man's prematurely white hair. Whenever a knife whistled to the black spot dead center in the target the men howled like animals while we children gulped in terror.

A white GI was taking a step back every time he hit the center of the target. Once again he took aim, but as the knife was about to spring from his hand he suddenly pivoted and the weapon slashed through the air toward us. We flattened ourselves, shrieking, against the wire fence surrounding the base. I felt a warm wetness between my legs. A moment later we lifted our pallid faces and saw the chuckling GI pointing at something behind us. We turned and saw a black cat rigid on its back, legs in the air, the knife stuck in its chest. The cat was the size of a small dog, probably one of the strays that were always getting into the garbage cans on the base. Its pointed whiskers were still trembling as we crowded around it. My big brother picked up the carcass and ran off. The rest of us took out after him. My wet underpants chafed.

When we were out of sight of the Americans' barracks my brother stopped, panting. He looked down at what he was holding, shuddered, and let

어지게 불러대었을 텐데 우리는 묵묵히 하늘 끝까지라도 이어질 것 같은 층계를 하나씩 올라갔다.

공원의 꼭대기에는 전설로 길이 남을 것이라는 상륙작전의 총지휘관이었던 노장군의 동상이 있었다. 그곳에서는 시가지 전체가 한눈에 들어왔다.

선창에 정박해 있는 크고 작은 배들의 깃발이 색종이처럼 조그맣게 팔랑이고 있는 사이 기중기는 쉬지 않고 화물을 물어 올렸다. 선창에서 멀찌감치 물러나 섬처럼, 늙은 잉어처럼 조용히 떠 있는 것은 외국 화물선일 것이다.

공원 뒤쪽의 성당에서는 끊임없이 종을 치고 있었다. 고양이를 바다에 던질 때부터, 아니 그 이전부터 우리 뒤를 따라오며 머리칼을 당기던 소리였다. 일정한 파문과 간격으로 한없이 계속되는, 극도로 절제되고 온갖 욕망과 성질을 단 하나의 동그라미로 단순화시킨 그 소리에는 한밤중 꿈 속에서 깨어나 문득 듣게 되는 여름밤의 먼 우레 소리, 혹은 깊은 밤 고달프게 달려가는 기차 바퀴 소리에서와 같은, 이해할 수 없는 두려움과 비밀스러움이 있었다.

수녀가 죽었나 봐.

누군가 말했다. 끊임없이 성당의 종이 울릴 때는 수녀가 고요히 죽어 가는 것이라는 것을 우리는 모두 알고 있

the cat drop. It fell to the ground with a thud.

"What did you bring *that* for?" one of the children demanded.

Thus challenged, my Little Napoleon of a brother pulled the knife from the cat's chest and wiped the blade on the grass. It was a folding knife, the blade sharp and pointed like an awl. He snapped the blade into place and put the knife in his pocket.

"Go get me a stick," he commanded.

One of us snapped off a branch from a tree we had planted the previous spring on Arbor Day and brought it to him.

Brother took off his belt and looped it around the cat's neck, then tied the end to the branch. Down the street we paraded, the cat splayed out behind my brother, its paws dragging along the ground and its weight bending the branch on his shoulder like a bow.

By the time we reached Chinatown the long summer day was waning. As the sun slanted toward the horizon the cat's shadow grew out endlessly from its midsection.

The flour mill workers walked past us on their way down the hill, their hair frosted with flour, their empty lunchboxes rattling.

었다.

철로 너머 제분 공장의 굴뚝에서 울컥울컥 토해 내는 검은 연기는 전쟁으로 부서진 도시의 하늘에 전진처럼 밀려들고 있었다.

전쟁사에 길이 남을 것이라는 치열했던 함포사격에도 제 모습을 고스란히 지니고 있는 것은 중국인 거리라고 불리는, 언덕 위의 이층집들과 우리 동네 낡은 적산 가옥들뿐이었다.

시가지 쪽에는 아직 햇빛이 머물러 있는데도 낙진처럼 내려앉는, 북풍에 실린 저탄장의 탄가루 때문일까, 중국인 거리는 연기가 서리듯 누눅한 어둠에 잠겨 들고 있었다.

시의 정상에서 조망하는 중국인 거리는, 검게 그을린 목조 적산 가옥 베란다에 널린 얼룩덜룩한 담요와 레이스의 속옷들은, 이 시의 풍물이었고 그림자였고 불가사의한 미소였으며 천칭의 한쪽 손에 얹혀 한없이 기우는 수은이었다. 또한 기우뚱 침몰하기 시작한 배의, 이미 물에 잠긴 고물이었다.

시의 동쪽 공설운동장에서 때이른 횃불이 피어 올랐다. 잔양 속에서 그것은 단지 하나의 흔들림, 너울대는 바람의 자락이었다. 그리고 사람들은 와아와아 함성을 질렀

We headed toward the pier, treading on each other's gigantic, frightening shadows and that of the cat's black, elongated carcass. And then I saw him again. The second-floor shutters were open and he was watching our procession. I couldn't fathom his gaze but I thought I saw sorrow, anger, and perhaps a subtle smile.

When we reached the pier Brother set the branch down and took the belt from around the cat's neck. Spitting in disgust, he cinched the belt around the waist of his pants, which were constantly threatening to fall down. Then he dropped the cat into the mass of garbage, empty bottles and rotting, white-bellied fish washing up against the embankment.

As we often did around sundown we decided to go to the park, where we liked to lie on our stomachs on the endless expanse of steps and look up the hoop skirts of the GIs' whores, exclaiming at the bare legs inside the bloated framework of whale tendon. Or we would loll on the grass and bellow one of the old standards an aging prostitute might sing to herself:

Looking back at my youth I see every step of the way stained with tears,

Looking back at my regrettable past I hear the bells

다. 체코, 폴란드, 물러가라, 꼭두각시, 괴뢰집단 물러가라, 와아와아. 여름 내내 햇빛이 걷히면 한 집에서 한 명씩 뽑혀 나간 사람들은 공설운동장에 모여 발을 구르며 외쳤다. 할머니는 돌아와 밤새 끙끙 허리를 앓았다.

중립국 감시위원단 중 공산측이 추천한 체코와 폴란드가(그들은 소련의 위성 국가입니다) 그들의 임무를 저버리고 유엔군측의 군사기밀을 캐내어 공산측에 보고하는 스파이가 되었기 때문입니다.

전체 조회에서 교장 선생님은 말했다.

무릎을 세우고 앉아 그 사이에 깊이 고개를 묻으면 함성은 병의 좁은 주둥이에 휘파람을 불어넣을 때처럼 아스라하게 웅웅대며 들려왔다. 땅속 깊숙이에서 울리는, 지층이 움직이는 소리, 해일의 전조로 미미하게 흔들리는 물살, 지붕 위를 핥으며 머무는 바람.

집으로 돌아왔을 때 어머니는 수채에 쭈그리고 앉아 으윽으윽 구역질을 하고 있었다. 임신의 징후였다. 이제 제발 동생을 그만 낳아 주었으면 좋겠다고 생각하며 나는 처음으로 여자의 동물적인 삶에 대해 동정했다. 어머니의 구역질에는 그렇게 비통하고 처절한 데가 있었다. 또 아이를 낳게 된다면 어머니는 죽게 될 것이다.

of Santa Maria.

But this time we walked up silently and deliberately toward the sky.

At the highest point in the park stood the bronze statue of the old general whose landing operation here just a few years ago was already inscribed in legend. From this spot the entire city could be seen. Boats and ships were moored at the pier, their flags fluttering like confetti, the jaws of a crane biting over and over into their cargo. Off in the distance floated a vessel that was probably a foreign freighter but looked more like an islet or a huge old carp.

The bell from the Catholic church behind us kept tolling. That tolling had been tugging at us ever since—no, even before—we'd thrown the cat into the sea. Producing endless waves of sound at precise intervals but confined to a single tone, simplifying every desire and state of mind into one basic harmony, the tolling evoked in me the awesomeness of a peal of thunder you hear on a summer evening when it wakes you from a dream, the mystery of train wheels rumbling through the deep of the night.

"A nun must have died."

When the bell kept tolling like this we thought it

밤이 깊어도 나는 잠을 잘 수가 없었다. 마악 생기기 시작한 젖망울을 할머니가 치마 말기를 뜯어 만들어 준 띠로 꽁꽁 동인 언니는 홑이불의 스침에도 젖이 아파 가슴을 싸쥐며 돌아누워 앓았다. 밤새도록 간단없이 들려오는 야경꾼의 딱딱이 소리, 화차의 바퀴 소리를 낱낱이 헤아리다가 날이 밝자 부두로 나갔다. 여전히 물결에 떠밀려 방죽에 부딪는 더러운 쓰레기와 썩은 생선들 사이에도, 더 멀리 닻 없이 떠 있는 폐선의 밑창에도 고양이는 없었다.

어느 먼 항구에서 아이들의 장대질에 의해 뼈가 무너진 허리 중동이를 허물며 끌어올려질지도 몰랐다.

가을로 접어들어도 빈대의 극성은 대단했다. 해가 퍼지면 우리는 다다미를 들어내어 베란다에 널어 습기를 말리고 빈대 알을 뒤졌다. 손목과 발목에 고무줄을 넣은 옷을 입고 자도 어느 틈에 빈대는 옷 속에서 스멀대며 비린 날콩 냄새를 풍겼다. 사람들은 전깃불이 나가는 열두시까지 대개 불을 켜 놓고 잠이 들었다. 불빛이 있으면 빈대가 덜 끓었기 때문이었다. 그러나 열두시를 기점으로 그것들은 다다미 짚 속에서, 벌어진 마루 틈에서 기어나와 총공격을 개시했다.

열은 잠 속에서 손톱을 세워 긁적이며 빈대와 싸우던

meant a nun was passing peacefully into the next world.

Across the railroad tracks a black stream spewed from the smokestack of the flour mill, surging into the sky above the war-ravaged city like dust rising from a battlefield.

The intense bombardment from the warships during the landing operation would long be remembered in the history of warfare, the grownups liked to say. About the only structures left intact were the old frame houses in our neighborhood, which had been seized from the Japanese at the end of the Pacific War, and the two-story houses on the hill in Chinatown.

While sunlight lingered in the western part of the city Chinatown was saturated with darkness, as if the smoke were smothering it or else the dust carried by the north wind from the coal yard was settling there like ash. Here at the highest point of the city we had a commanding view of Chinatown and the colored blankets and lace underwear on the balconies of the sooty houses seized from the Japanese. These were the scenes, the underside, the mysterious smile of this city. Part of me would always be weighed down by these images. To me,

나는 문득 나무토막이 부서지는 둔탁하고 메마른 소리에 눈을 떴다. 오빠는 어느새 바지를 주워 입고 총알처럼 계단을 뛰어 내려가고 있었다. 바깥에서는 갑작스런 소음이 끓었다. 무슨 사건이 일어났구나, 나는 가슴을 두근대며 베란다로 나갔다. 불이 나간 지 오래되어 깜깜한 거리, 치옥이네 집과 우리 집 앞을 메우며 사람들이 가득 와글와글 떠들고 있었다. 뒤미처 늘어선 집들의 유리문이 드르륵 열리고 베란다로 나온 사람들이 무슨 일이냐고 소리쳤다. 죽었다는 소리가 웅성거림 속에 계시처럼 들렸다. 모여선 사람들은 이어부르는 노래를 하듯 입에서 입으로 죽었다는 말을 옮기며 진저리를 치거나 겹겹이 둘러싼 틈으로 고개를 쑤셔넣었다. 나는 턱을 달달 떨어대며 치옥이네 집 이 층 시커멓게 열린 매기 언니의 방과 러닝셔츠 바람으로 베란다의 난간을 짚고 아래를 내려다보고 이는 검둥이를 보았다.

잠시 후 요란한 사이렌을 울리며 미군 지프차가 달려왔다. 겹겹이 진을 친 사람들이 순식간에 양쪽으로 갈라졌다. 헤드라이트의 쏟아질 듯 밝은 불빛 속에 매기 언니가 반듯이 누워 있었다. 염색한, 길고 숱 많은 머리털이 흩어져 후광처럼 얼굴을 감싸고 있었다. 위에서 던져 버렸다

Chinatown and my neighborhood were the flooded stern of a listing ship about to sink.

Torches, lit too early in the evening, flared at the public playfield in the eastern part of the city. Framed by the last traces of sunlight the flames swayed and flickered in the remnants of the wind. A crowd was crying out, "Czechoslovakia go home! Poland go home! Puppet regimes go home!" For the entire summer one member from each household had to report to the playfield at sundown to join the slogan-shouting, foot-stamping throng. Grandmother would return from these rallies complaining of pain in her lower back and groan all night.

One morning during assembly our principal explained the reason for the protests. Czechoslovakia and Poland, satellites of the Soviet Union, had forsworn their obligations as members of the neutral-nations peacekeeping force by attempting to uncover U.N. military secrets to pass on to the communist side.

If I buried my head between my knees the outcry from the playfield became a distant hum, kind of like the sound I could make blowing across the narrow mouth of an empty bottle. A sound I associated with the earth groaning deep below the surface, a

는군.

검둥이는 술에 취해 있었다. 엠피가 검둥이의 벗은 몸에 군복을 걸쳤다. 검둥이는 단추를 풀어헤치고 낄낄대며 지프차에 실려 떠났다.

입의 한 귀로 흘러내리는 물을 짜증을 내는 법도 없이 찬찬히 닦아주며 치옥이는 제니에게 물을 먹이고 있었다. 아무리 물을 먹여도 제니의 딸꾹질은 멎지 않았다.

고아원에 가게 될 거야.

치옥이가 말했다. 봄이 되면 매기 언니는 미국에 가게 될 거야, 검둥이가 국제결혼을 해 준대, 라고 말하던 때처럼 조금 시무룩한 말투였다. 그 무렵 매기 언니는 행복해 보였다. 침대에 걸터앉은 검둥이의 발을 닦아 주는 매기 언니의, 물들인 머리를 높이 틀어올려 깨끗한 목덜미를 물끄러미 보노라면 화장을 지운, 눈썹이 없는 얼굴로 나를 돌아보며 상냥하게 손짓했다. 들어와, 괜찮아.

제니는 성당의 고아원에 갔어.

이틀 후 치옥이는 빨갛게 부은 눈을 사납게 찡그리며 말했다. 매기 언니의 동생이 와서 매기 언니의 짐을 모조리 실어 가며 제니만 달랑 남겨 놓았다는 것이다. 치옥이네 이 층은 꽤 오랫동안 비어 있었다. 그러나 나는 치옥이

faint ripple foreshadowing a tidal wave, a lingering breeze licking the roofs of houses.

At home I found Mother retching beside the drain in the yard. For the first time I empathized with the brutish life that women had to live. There was something pathetic and harrowing about Mother's retching, and this symptom of her pregnancy made me plead silently with her to produce no more brothers and sisters for me. I was afraid she would die if she gave birth again.

I couldn't get to sleep until well into the night. My older sister had bound her emerging breasts with a waistband Grandmother tore from a skirt, and because they were sensitive even to the touch of the sheets she was tossing and turned, hands crossed over her chest and moaning. Lying awake I tried to count the number of times the night guards tapped their sticks together to signal their approach and the number of wheels of the freight trains that passed by. At daybreak I went back to the pier. The dead cat was nowhere to be seen among the garbage and rotting fish washing up against the embankment, nor was it beneath an abandoned boat I spotted drifting a short distance offshore. Perhaps by now some children in a distant port

네 집에 숙제를 하러 가거나 놀러가지 않았다.

아침마다 길에서 큰소리로 치옥이를 불렀다.

또 아이를 낳게 된다면 어머니는 죽을 것이라는 예감이 신념처럼 굳어 가고 있었지만 어머니의 배는 치마 밑에서 조심스럽게 불러 가고 있었다. 대신 매운 손맛과 나지막하고 독한 욕설로 나날이 정정해지던 할머니가 쓰러졌다. 빨래를 하다가 모로 쓰러진 후 제정신이 돌아오지 않는 것이다. 할머니의 등에 업혀 살던 막내동생은 언니의 차지가 되었다.

대소변을 받아내게 되자 어머니와 아버지는 할머니를 할아버지가 있는 시골로 보내는 것에 합의를 보았다.

이십 년도 가는 수가 있대요. 중풍이란 돌도 삭인다니까요.

어머니는 작게 소곤거렸다. 그리고는 조금 큰소리로, 미우니 고우니 해도 늘그막에는 영감님 곁이 제일이에요 했고, 이어 택시를 대절해서 모셔야 해요 하고 크게 말했다.

할머니는 다시 아기가 되었다. 나는 치옥이가 제니에게 하듯 아무도 없을 때면 할머니의 방에 들어가 머리를 빗기고 물을 입에 떠 넣기도 하고 가끔 쉬이를 했는지 속옷을 헤치고 기저귀 속에 살그머니 손끝을 대어 보기도

were dragging its shapeless body around at the end of a pole.

Autumn drew near but the bedbugs flourished as never before. When the sun shone full on the balcony we took the tatamis outside to dry and scoured the wooden floors of our rooms for the eggs. Though our pajamas had elastic cuffs, the bedbugs managed to crawl inside, making us itch and producing the smell of raw beans. The electricity stayed on until midnight and we usually went to sleep with the lights on because they kept the bugs away. But when the lights went out the bugs swarmed out of the tatami straw and the cracks in the floor and launched an all-out attack.

One night when I was half asleep and scratching away at the bugs I was awakened by a *thunk*—it sounded like someone splitting wood. Before I knew it my older brother had thrown on his pants and shot down the stairs. I could tell from the hubbub on the street that something had happened. My heart quickened and I went out on the balcony. The electricity was off and it was pitch dark but I could make out the noisy crowd that had filled the street between our house and Ch'i-ok's. Sliding glass doors scraped open on the balconies above, our

했다.

할머니가 떠나는 날 어머니는 할머니의 옷을 벗기고 새로 빤 옷을 갈아입혔다.

평생 자식을 실어보지도 못한 몸이라 아직 몸매가 이렇게 고우시구나.

할아버지가, 할머니의 동생인 작은 할머니와 그 사이에 낳은 자식들과 살고 있는 시골에 할머니를 모셔다 놓고 온 아버지는 한숨을 쉬며 더듬더듬 말했다.

못할 짓을 한 것 같다, 그 집에서 누가 달가워하겠어, 개밥에 도토리지. 그런데 부부라는 게 뭔지……. 글쎄 의식이 하나도 없는 양반이 펄떡펄떡 열불이 나는 가슴을 풀어헤치고 영감님 손을 끌어 당겨 거기에 얹더라니까…….

그러게 내가 뭐랬어요, 역시 보내드리길 잘했지. 평생 서리서리 뭉쳐 둔 한인 걸요.

어머니는 할머니가 쓰던 반닫이의 고리를 열었다. 평소에 할머니가 만지지도 못하게 하던 것이라 우리들의 길게 뺀 목도 어머니의 손길을 따라 움직였다. 어머니는 차곡차곡 쌓인 옷가지들을 하나씩 들어내어 방바닥에 놓았다. 다리 부분을 줄여 할머니가 입던 아버지의 헌 내의, 허드

neighbors shouting questions to those below. Among the hum of voices the word "dead" came to my ears like a revelation. The word passed from mouth to mouth like a round, some people shuddering in disgust, others poking their heads through the layers of onlookers. I felt my chin tremble as I looked across the street and saw that the door to Maggie's room was open. The darky, dressed in an undershirt, was looking down on the street from the balcony, his hands resting on the railing.

I heard the wail of a siren and the next moment an American army jeep arrived. Instantly the crowd parted and there lying in the street was Maggie, drenched in the brightness of the jeep's headlights. Her long, thick hair covered her face and was strewn every which way, like solar flares. "He threw her into the street," somebody said.

The darky was drunk. The MPs got him into his uniform and as they loaded him into the jeep, his shirt unbuttoned, he chuckled.

The next day I found Ch'i-ok giving water to Jennie. The little girl had the hiccups. Ch'i-ok patiently wiped the moisture trickling from the corner of Jenny's mouth. But no amount of water could stop make the hiccups.

레로 입던 몸뻬 따위가 바닥에 쌓였다. 그리고 항라, 숙고사 같은 옛날 천의 옷이 나왔다. 점차 어머니의 손길에 끌려 나온, 지난날 할머니가 한두 번쯤 입고 아껴 넣어 두었을 옷가지들을 보는 사이 비로소 이제 할머니는 돌아오지 않는다, 이런 옷들을 입을 날이 없을 것이라는 생각이 들어 가슴 밑바닥에 바람이 지나가듯 서늘해졌다. 할머니는 언제 저 옷들을 입었을까, 언제 다시 입기 위해 아끼고 아껴 깊이 넣어 둔 걸까.

마지막으로 어머니는 수달피 배자를 들어내고 밑바닥을 더듬었다. 그리고 손수건에 단단히 싼 조그만 물건을 꺼냈다. 어머니의 손길이 그대로 잽싸게 움직이는 동안 우리 형제들은 숨을 죽여 뚫어지게 그것을 바라보았다.

어머니는 의아한 얼굴로 눈살을 찌푸려 손수건 속을 들여다보았다. 그 속에는 동강이 난 비취 반지, 퍼렇게 녹이 슬어 금방 부스러져 버릴 듯한 구리 혁대 버클, 왜정 때의 백동전 몇 닢, 어느 옷에 달았던 것인지 모를 크고 작은 몇 개의 단추, 색실 토막 따위가 들어 있었다.

노친네도 참, 깨진 비취는 사금파리나 다름없어.

어머니는 혀를 차며 그것을 다시 손수건에 싸서 빈 반닫이에 던져 놓았다. 내의 따위 속옷은 걸렛감으로 내어

"They're going to put her in an orphanage," Ch'i-ok said. She sounded a bit sulky, like on the day she told me that Maggie was bound for America in the spring—the darky had decided to marry her.

Maggie had looked happy then. Once I found her washing the darky's feet as he sat on the edge of the bed. Her dyed hair was piled high on her head and as I stared at the clean nape of her neck she turned to me. Without makeup she looked like she had no eyebrows. She gently beckoned me. "It's okay. Come on in."

"Jennie went to the Catholic orphanage," Ch'i-ok told me with a fierce scowl two days later. Her eyes were red and puffy. A younger sister of Maggie's had come to pack up the dead woman's belongings. Maggie's room remained empty for some time. But I didn't go up there to do homework or play with Ch'i-ok anymore. Instead I called to her from the street on my way to school every morning.

As Mother's stomach continued to swell almost imperceptibly beneath her skirt I grew more and more convinced she wouldn't survive another birth. As it turned out, the one who failed was Grandmother, whose stinging hands and pungent, vicious curses had seemed to make her healthier by the

놓고 옷가지들은 어머니의 장에 옮겨 놓았다. 수달피는 고급품이어서 목도리로 고쳐 쓰겠다고 했다.

다음 날 나는 아무도 몰래 반닫이를 열고 손수건 뭉치를 꺼냈다. 그러고는 공원으로 올라가 장군의 동상에서부터 숲 쪽으로 할머니의 나이 수대로 예순다섯 발자국을 걸어 숲의 다섯 번째 오리나무 밑에 깊이 묻었다.

겨울의 끝 무렵 우리는 할머니의 부음을 들었다. 택시에 실려 떠난 지 두 계절 만이었다.

산원을 앞둔 어머니는 새삼스럽게 할머니가 쓰던, 이제는 우리들의 해진 옷가지들이 뒤죽박죽 되는 대로 쑤셔 박힌 반닫이를 어루만지며 울었다.

저녁 내내 아무도 찾아내지 못할, 골방의 잡동사니들 틈에서 숨을 죽이고 있던 나는 밤이 되자 공원으로 올라갔다. 아주 깜깜했지만 나는 예순 다섯 걸음을 걷지 않고도 정확히 숲의 다섯 번째 오리나무를 찾을 수 있었다.

깊은 땅 속에서 두 계절을 묻혀 있던 손수건은 썩은 지푸라기처럼 축축하게 손가락 사이에서 묻어났다. 동강 난 비취 반지와 녹슨 버클, 몇 닢 백동전의 흙을 털어 가만히 손 안에 쥐었다. 똑같았다. 모두가 전과 다름없었다. 잠시의 온기와 이내 되살아나는 차가움.

day. One morning she collapsed while doing the laundry. She never recovered. My baby brother, who had practically lived on her back, became my big sister's responsibility.

When Grandmother began needing a bedpan, Mother and Father agreed to move her to the countryside, where Grandfather lived.

"The effects can last twenty years," Mother whispered to Father. "That's why they say a stroke can melt a rock." And in a slightly louder voice, "When you're old there's only one place to be, and that's next to your husband, whether you love him or hate him." Finally, in a loud tone, "We'd better arrange a taxi for her."

Grandmother was as helpless as a baby. As Ch'i-ok had done with Jennie, I would go into Grandmother's room when no one else was home and comb her hair and give her water to drink and sometimes I gently checked her diaper.

On the day Grandmother was to leave, Mother dressed her in clean clothes and then reported, "She still has her figure because she never had children."

And then Father left with her for the village where Grandfather lived with her younger sister and their children. "I don't feel right about it," Father sighed

나는 다시 손 안의 물건들을 나무 밑에 묻고 흙을 덮었다. 손의 흙을 털고 나무 밑을 꼭꼭 밟아 다진 뒤 일정한 보폭을 유지하는 데 신경을 쓰며 장군의 동상을 향해 걸었다. 예순 번을 세자 동상이었다. 나는 고개를 갸웃했다. 분명히 두 계절 전 예순 다섯걸음의 거리였다. 앞으로 다시 두 계절이 지나면 쉰 걸음으로 닿을 수가 있을까, 다시 일 년이 지나면, 그리고 십 년이 지나면 단 한 걸음으로 날듯 닿을 수가 있을까.

아직 겨울이고 깊은 밤이어서 나는 굳이 사람들의 눈을 피하지 않고도 쉽게 장군의 동상에 올라갈 수 있었다. 키를 넘는, 위가 잘려진 정사면체의 받침돌에 손톱을 박고 기어올라 장군의 배 위에 모아 쥔 망원경 부분에 발을 딛고 불빛이 듬성듬성 박힌 시가지를 내려다보았다. 지난해 여름 전진처럼 자욱이 피어오르던 함성은 이제 들려오지 않았다. 다만 조용했다. 귀 기울여 어둠 속에 부드럽게 흐르는 소리를 좇노라면 땅 속 가장 깊은 곳에서 숨어 흐르는 수맥이라도 손 끝에 닿을 것 같은 조용함이었다.

나는 깜깜하게 엎드린 바다를 보았다. 동지나해로부터 밤새워 불어오는 바람, 바람에 실린 해조류의 냄새를 깊이 들이마셨다. 그리고 중국인 거리, 언덕 위 이층집의 덧

when he returned. He spoke falteringly. "I don't think they'll be happy with her. She'll be a thorn in their side. You know, it's amazing—I thought she wouldn't know anyone but apparently she recognized your father—she spread her jacket, took his hand, and placed it on her chest. Can you imagine how frustrated she must have been all these years? 'Till death do us part'—makes you wonder."

"There was a lifetime of bitterness inside that woman," said Mother. "But didn't I tell you? We did the right thing sending her there."

Mother decided to open Grandmother's clothing chest—something Grandmother had never let any of us touch. Eagerly we followed the movement of Mother's hands. One by one she removed the neatly folded articles of clothing and placed them on the floor. Out came Father's old long underwear, which Grandmother had hemmed for her own use, and the Japanese-style baggy pants she had worn around the house, and clothes made from sheer silk and from thick, glossy silk and from other fabrics woven in the traditional way. As Mother continued to reach into the chest for clothing worn perhaps once or twice in a lifetime I finally realized that Grandmother was not coming back, that the days

문이 열리며 쏟아져 나와 장방형으로 내려앉는 불빛과 드러나는 창백한 얼굴을 보았다. 차가운 공기 속에 연한 봄의 숨결이 숨어 있었다.

나는 따스한 핏속에서 돋아오르는 순을, 참을 수 없는 근지러움으로 감지했다.

인생이란…….

나는 중얼거렸다. 그러나 뒤를 이을 어떤 적절한 말도 떠오르지 않았다. 알 수 없는, 다만 복잡하고 분명치 않은 색채로 뒤범벅된 혼란에 가득찬 어제와 오늘의 수없이 다가올 내일들을 뭉뚱거릴 한마디의 말을 찾을 수 있을까.

다시 봄이 되고 나는 육 학년이 되었다. 오빠는 어디서인지 강아지를 한 마리 얻어와 길을 들이는 중이었다. 할머니가 없는 집 안에 개는 멋대로 터럭을 날리고 똥을 쌌다.

나는 일 년 동안 키가 한 뼘이나 자랐고 언니가 쓰던, 장미가 수놓여진 옥스퍼드 천의 가방을 들게 된 것은 지난해부터였다.

우리는 겨우내 화차에서 석탄을 훔치고 밤이면 여전히 거리를 쥐 떼처럼 몰려다니며 소란을 떨었으나 때때로 골방에 틀어박혀 대본집에서 빌려 온 연애소설 따위를 읽기도 했다.

when she might have worn such clothes were gone, and I felt a chill sweep through the depths of my heart. When had she worn those clothes? And for what special occasion had she stored them deep inside the chest?

The last article of clothing was an otter vest. Mother then groped along the bottom of the chest and produced a tightly wrapped handkerchief. With bated breath we fixed our eyes on Mother's nimble fingers.

With a quizzical expression Mother looked inside the handkerchief. A jade ring broken in two, a tarnished copper belt buckle that looked about to crumble, a few nickel coins from the Japanese occupation, buttons of various sizes that might once have been attached to clothing, some colored threads—such were the contents.

"Really, Mother!" she clucked. Saving broken jade is like saving bits of pottery." Mother rewrapped the objects and tossed the handkerchief into the empty chest. After setting aside the long underwear and other underclothing to use as rags she moved the remainder of the clothing to her own chest. The otter fur was of high quality, she told us—she would use it as a muffler.

토요일이어서 오전 수업뿐이었다. 회충약을 먹는 날이니 아침을 굶고 와요, 배가 부른 회충은 약을 받아먹지 않아요.

사람들은 이제는 집을 훨씬 덜 지었으나 해인초 끓이는 냄새는 빠지지 않는 염색물감처럼 공기를 노랗게 착색시키고 있었다. 햇빛이 노랗게 끓은 거리에, 자주 멈춰 서서 침을 뱉으며 나는 중얼거렸다.

회충이 지랄을 하나 봐.

치옥이는 깡통에 파마약을 풀고 있었다.

제분 공장에 다니던 치옥이의 아버지가 피댓줄에 감겨 다리가 끊긴 후 치옥이의 부모가 치옥이를 삼거리의 미장원에 맡기고 이 거리를 떠난 것은 지난겨울이었다. 나는 매일 학교를 오가는 길에 미장원 앞을 지나치며 유리문을 통해 치옥이를 보았다. 치옥이는 자꾸 기어올라 가는 작은 스웨터를 끌어당겨 바지허리 위로 드러나는 맨살을 가리며 미장원 바닥에 떨어진 머리칼을 쓸고 있었다.

나는 미장원 앞을 떠났다. 수천의 깃털이 날아오르듯 거리는 노란 햇빛으로 가득차 있었다. 언제였지, 언제였지, 나는 좀체로 기억나지 않는 먼 꿈을 되살리려는 안타까움으로 고개를 흔들며 집을 향해 걸었다. 그리고 집 앞

The next day I sneaked into Grandmother's chest and retrieved the wrapped-up handkerchief and took it to the park, where I walked sixty-five paces from the statue of the general—one step for each year Grandmother had lived. The last step brought me to an alder—the fifth tree into a grove—and there I dug deep and buried the handkerchief and its contents.

Toward the end of winter word arrived that Grandmother had passed on. It was just the previous summer that she had left in the taxi. Mother, now in her ninth month, did something uncharacteristic: she began crying as she caressed Grandmother's clothing chest, which was stuffed topsy-turvy with all of our threadbare clothing.

That evening I hid among the odds and ends in the back room, where no one could find me, and when everyone had gone to bed I went to the park. The sky was black but I found the fifth alder tree without having to count to sixty-five steps.

The damp handkerchief, buried deep in the ground for two seasons, stuck to my palm like rotten straw. I brushed the dirt off the halves of the ring, the tarnished belt buckle, and the coins and held them tenderly. They felt exactly the same.

에 이르러 언덕 위의 이층집 열린 덧창을 바라보았다. 그가 창으로 상체를 내밀어 나를 손짓해 부르고 있었다.

내가 끌리듯 언덕 위를 올라가자 그는 창문에서 사라졌다. 그리고 잠시 후 닫힌 대문을 무겁게 밀고 나왔다. 코허리가 낮고 누런 빛의 얼굴에 여전히 알 수 없는 미소를 띠고 있었다.

그는 내게 종이꾸러미를 내밀었다. 내가 받아들자 그는 몸을 돌려 안으로 들어갔다. 열린 문으로 어둡고 좁은, 안채로 들어가는 통로와 갑자기 나타나는 볕바른 마당과, 걸음을 옮길 때마다 투명한 맨발에 찰랑대며 묻어 오르는 햇빛을 보았다.

나는 골방에 들어가 문을 잠근 뒤 종이뭉치를 끌렀다. 속에 든 것은 중국인들이 명절 때 먹는 세 가지 색의 물감을 들인 빵과 용이 장식된 엄지손가락만 한 등이었다.

나는 그것들을 금이 가서 쓰지 않는 빈 항아리 속에 넣었다. 안방에서는 어머니가 산고의 비명을 지르고 있었으나 나는 이 층으로 올라갔다. 그리고 숨바꼭질을 할 때처럼 몰래 벽장 속으로 숨어들어갔다. 한낮이어도 벽장 속은 한점의 빛도 들지 않아 어두웠다. 나는 차라리 죽여 줘라고 부르짖는 어머니의 비명과 언제부터인가 울리기 시작

They warmed up in my hand but soon the cold would return.

I replaced the objects in their grave beneath the tree. After I had tamped the dirt down and brushed off my hands I started back toward the statue, taking even steps. At the count of sixty I was there. Hmm—it had been sixty-five steps the previous summer. Did this mean it would be fifty paces next summer? And a year later, or ten years later, would one giant step take me there?

Since it was winter and late at night there was no one to give me a disapproving look if I climbed the statue. So I clawed my way onto the pedestal and then to the binoculars that the general held against his stomach. From there I looked down on the city with its sprinkling of lights. The outcries of the previous summer, swelling like dust from a battlefield, were gone. Now it was still. As I strained to listen to the sounds flowing gently through the darkness I felt as if I were tapping an undiscovered vein of water near the core of the earth.

The sea was a black plane. I drank in the wind that had been blowing all night from the East China Sea, and the seaweed smell it carried. I saw the oblong light framed by the open shutter of the two-

한 종소리를 들으며 죽음과도 같은 낮잠에 빠져들어갔다.

내가 낮잠에서 깨어났을 때 어머니는 지독한 난산이었지만 여덟 번째 아이를 밀어내었다. 어두운 벽장 속에서 나는 이해할 수 없는 절망감과 막막함으로 어머니를 불렀다. 그리고 옷 속에 손을 넣어 거미줄처럼 온몸을 끈끈하게 죄고 있는 후덥덥한 열기를, 그 열기의 정체를 찾아내었다.

초조(初潮)였다.

『유년의 뜰』, 문학과지성사, 1998(1979)

story house on the Chinatown hill and imagined a pale face revealed within it. I felt the soft breath of spring hiding in the chilly air.

Something was budding in my warm blood, something unbearably ticklish.

"Life is..." I murmured. But I couldn't find the right word. Was there a single word for today and yesterday, with their jumble of indistinguishable, all too complicated colors, a word to embrace all the tomorrows?

And then it was spring again and I was a sixth-grader. One day my older brother brought home a puppy. With Grandmother gone it had the run of the house, pooping and shedding anywhere it pleased.

I had grown the better part of a foot in the past twelve months, and last year I'd started using my older sister's oxford-cloth school bag embroidered with roses.

All winter long my rat pack and I had sneaked coal from the freight trains and as always had run wild through the streets. Occasionally I had closeted myself in the back room at home to read popular romances and such.

One Saturday afternoon I was on my way home

from school—Saturday being the one day when we didn't have classes in the afternoon. "Tomorrow's worm medicine day, so be sure to skip breakfast," our teacher had reminded us on Friday. "The worms won't take the medicine on a full belly."

There was much less rebuilding in the neighborhood now, but Corsican weed was still boiled and the smell still seemed to dye the air yellow.

In the simmering yellow sunlight I frequently stopped to spit. "Feels like the worms are going nuts," I muttered once again.

I saw Ch'i-ok mixing permanent-wave solution in a can in the beauty shop at the three-way intersection. Her father had lost a leg in a conveyor belt at the flour mill and had moved away with his wife the previous winter. Ch'i-ok stayed behind and was living with the people who ran the beauty shop. Every day I passed it on my way to and from school and saw her through the glass door. Usually I found her sweeping in between pulling down her small sweater, which constantly rode up her back to reveal her bare waist.

I walked past the beauty shop. The yellow sunlight filling the street looked like thousands of feathers soaring into the air. When was it? Shaking my head in irritation I tried to revive a distant, barely remembered dream. When was it? I continued toward home, and when I arrived I looked at the open window of the two-story house on the hill. He was leaning partway out the window, beckoning me.

I started up the hill, drawn as if by a magnet, and he disappeared from the window. A moment later he heaved open the gate to the house and there he was. His yellow, flat-nosed face still wore that mysterious smile.

He offered me something wrapped in paper and when I accepted it he went back inside. Through the open gate I saw a narrow, shaded front walk and a yard with so much sun it startled me, sunlight dancing and darting on the limpid skin of his feet with every step he took.

At home I went into the back room, locked the door, and opened the package. Inside was bread dyed in three colors, the kind the Chinese ate on their holidays, and a thumb-size lantern decorated with a plastic dragon.

I hid these items in a cracked jar that no one used. Mother was in labor in my parents' room, but instead of looking in on her I went upstairs and sneaked into the storage cabinet like I did when playing hide and seek. It was midday but not a ray of light entered my hiding place. As I listened to Mother screaming that she wanted to die I realized the church bell was tolling and then I fell into a sleep that was like death itself.

I learned later that by the time I awoke, Mother had pushed her eighth child into the world after a terrible labor. In the darkness of the cabinet a sense of helplessness and despair came over me and I called out to her. I felt inside my underwear and finally I understood the humid fever that had been closing about me like a spider web.

My first menstrual flow had begun.

Translated by Bruce and Ju-chan Fulton

해설

Afterword

전후 유년 시절의 한 풍경과 소녀의 성장

박진영(문학평론가)

「중국인 거리」(1979)는 한국전쟁 이후 항구 도시를 배경으로, 한 소녀가 겪는 일련의 사건을 내밀하게 묘사하고 있는 작품이다. 이 소설은 1950년에 일어난 한국전쟁 직후 인천의 중국인 거리에 사는 한 소녀를 주인공으로 하고 있다. 아홉 살짜리 소녀(나)와 그의 가족은 시골에서 이주해 온 가난한 피난민들이다. '나'는 도시에 대한 호기심과 기대를 갖고 인천에 도착하지만, 그곳은 내가 꿈꾸어 온 도회지와는 전혀 다른 곳이었다. '오색의 비눗방울 혹은 말로만 듣던 먼 나라의 크리스마스트리'의 연상과는 무관하게, 전쟁으로 부서진 건물들과 똑같은 모양의 목조 이층집들이 늘어 선 거리는 지저분하고 초라할 뿐이었다.

A Landscape In the Postwar Days and a Girl's Coming Of Age

Pak Jin-young (literary critic)

Chinatown (1979) is set in the port city of Incheon in the aftermath of the Korean War (1950~53) and intimately depicts a series of events experienced by the protagonist, a nine-year-old girl. The protagonist ("I") and her family are refugees, poor migrants from the countryside. The girl arrives in Incheon with great expectations of city life, but finds it very different from what she had dreamed. For a child living in the country, a city is always associated with things like "the rainbow-colored soap bubbles or else the Christmas trees we'd heard about." However, the city the girl moves to is dirty and shabby, with its streets lined with run-down build-

뿐만 아니라 집을 짓는 데 사용되는 해인초 끓이는 냄새가 늘 머리를 아프게 하고, 할머니의 푸념처럼 석탄 가루가 항상 날려 빨래를 널기 힘든 곳이 바로 중국인 거리였다. 전쟁의 상처가 남아 있는 거칠고 각박한 그곳에서 소녀와 그 가족은 중국인, 미군, 피난민들과 함께 어울려 살아간다. 작가는 특히 노란색의 색채 이미지와 "유년의 기억"을 떠올리게 하는 후각적 이미지를 통해 피난지에서의 생활을 묘사하고 있다.

'나'는 그곳에서 가난한 아이들과 함께 제분 공장의 밀가루를 훔치고, 화차의 석탄을 훔쳐 간식으로 바꾸어 먹는다. 중국인 거리에 사는 아이들은 순수한 동심을 표상하지 않는다. 그들은 피난지에서의 어수선하고 가난한 생활에 지쳐 각박해진 '작은 어른'일 뿐이다. 나는 정육점에 가서 어머니가 주의를 준 대로 "애라고 조금 주세요?"라고 선수를 치고, 이발소에 가서는 이발사가 머리 모양을 주문한 대로 자르지 않자 "그러길래 왜 아저씨는 이발만 열심히 하지 잡담을 하느냔 말예요"라고 악을 쓰며 어른을 놀린다. 중국인 거리에서 나는 아름다운 유년기를 보내는 대신 영악하고 조숙한 아이로 성장해 나간다.

또한 소녀의 눈으로 바라보는 어른들의 세계 역시 아름

ings and identically shaped, two-story wooden houses.

Further, the Chinatown where the girl's family settles reeks of boiling Corsican weed, an algae used in building houses, which always gives her a headache; and drifting coal powder stains the wash hung out to dry, as her grandmother complains. The child protagonist and her family live in this rough and inhumane, war-stricken town along with Chinese, American, and other displaced people. The author describes life in this place of refuge through the yellow tints and strong smells that conjure up the narrator's "childhood memory."

The girl, along with other poor children, steals flour from a mill and coal from freight trains to trade for snacks. The children in Chinatown do not represent innocence; instead they are "little grown-ups" hardened by the unstable and abject life of refugees. The girl goes to the butcher's and makes a preemptive wisecrack by saying, "Are you only giving me this much because I'm a child?" as instructed by her mother. While getting a haircut, when she finds the result not to her liking, she immediately snaps at the barber, "Why can't you concentrate on cutting hair instead of gabbing with everybody?" In

답지 않은 모습이다. 소녀에게는 "난 커서 양갈보가 될 테야"라고 늘 말하는, 치옥이라는 친구가 있다. 치옥이네 이층에는 흑인 남자와 매기 언니가 사는데, 치옥이와 나는 매기 언니의 방에서 '초록색의 액체'를 몰래 마시기도 하고, 이국적인 비밀스러운 물건들을 보며 신기해한다. 소설에는 한편 호기심의 대상인 아편쟁이, 밀수업자 중국인과 칼로 다트 놀이를 하는 미군, 이층집 창문으로 밖을 내다보는 젊은 중국인 남자, 매기 언니의 딸인 제니, 계속해서 동생을 낳는 어머니와 어머니의 서모인 할머니 등이 등장한다. 「중국인 거리」는 이들을 통해 전쟁 후 혼란 속에서 살아가는 어른들의 어두운 모습을 아이의 눈으로 이야기하고 있다.

이 가운데 소녀가 겪는 중요한 사건은 매기 언니와 할머니의 '죽음'이다. 흑인과 결혼해 미국에 갈 거라던 매기 언니는 막상 술 취한 그에 의해 이 층에서 내동댕이쳐지며, 할머니는 쓰러져 시골에 보내지지만 얼마 안 있어 죽고 만다. 또한 제니는 고아원에 보내지고, 치옥이는 공장에서 다리가 잘린 아버지와 의붓엄마가 중국인 거리를 떠나면서 미장원에 맡겨진다. 뿐만 아니라 고양이 새끼들의 죽음, 고양이의 죽음, 수녀의 죽음을 암시하는 종소리 등

this Chinatown, children are shrewd and precocious.

From the girl's perspective, there is nothing beautiful about the world of adults. She has a friend, a girl named Ch'i-ok, who always says, "I'm going to be a GI's whore when I grow up." An African-American man and a Korean woman called Maggie live on the second floor of Ch'i-oks house. The protagonist and Ch'i-ok sneak into Maggie's room, drink some "green liquid," and wonder at the exotic, mysterious things they find. There are other characters in the story who attract the protagonist's attention: an opium addict; American soldiers and a Chinese smuggler playing darts with knives; a young Chinese man looking out a window from the second floor; Maggie's daughter Jennie; the protagonist's mother who keeps having babies; the grandmother who is a concubine of the protagonist's maternal grandfather; and so forth. Using these characters as observed by the nine-year-old, the author portrays the dark nature of adult lives during the turbulent aftermath of the Korean War.

One of the main motifs of the story is the death of Maggie and of the protagonist's grandmother. Maggie, who is planning to marry the African-American

에서 죽음과 소멸의 이미지가 반복적으로 나타난다.

이러한 죽음과 이별을 겪는 다른 한편 소녀는 생명의 탄생과 성장을 경험하기도 한다. 나는 계속해서 아이를 낳는 어머니의, '여자의 동물적인 삶에 대해 동정'하기도 하지만 소설에서는 일곱 번째, 여덟 번째 동생이 새롭게 태어나고, 화자 역시 '초조(초경)'를 치름으로써 사춘기의 나이에 접어들게 된다. 「중국인 거리」에는 죽음의 사건과 함께 삶과 생명의 양면성이 공존하고 있다. 소녀는 이 둘을 통해 혼란과 어두움의 세계뿐만 아니라 삶의 온전한 의미에 보다 접근하게 된다고 할 수 있다. 「중국인 거리」는 이처럼 전쟁이 휩쓸고 간 자리에 남은 상처와 함께 그 속에서 세상의 빛과 어두움을 알아 나가는 소녀의 모습을 통해 전후의 한 풍경을 성장 서사로 담고 있는 작품이다.

soldier and move to the United States with him, is thrown from the second-floor window by her drunken future husband. The girl's grandmother dies after she has a stroke and is sent back to her home village. Jennie is sent to an orphanage. Ch'i-ok is left at a beauty parlor when her father, whose leg is maimed in an accident at the factory where he works, leaves Chinatown with his wife, Ch'i-ok's stepmother. There are other recurring images of death and loss throughout the story such as the deaths of kittens and a mother cat, the death of a nun implied by the sound of a church bell, and so on.

Aside from deaths and separations, the girl also experiences birth and growth. She empathized with the brutish life that women had to live, especially her mother who is constantly bearing children; however, after the birth of her eighth younger sibling, she reaches puberty with her first menses. The story *Chinatown* deals with the duality of life and death, through which the protagonist gains access not only to the realm of darkness and confusion but also to a deeper understanding of life. *Chinatown*, a lyrical description of the landscape of postwar Korean society, tells us about a girl becoming aware of the light and darkness of a world suffering from the wounds inflicted by war.

비평의 목소리
Critical Acclaim

이러한 소설에서는 묘사 하나, 단어 하나라도 조금만 소홀히 읽게 되면 우리가 읽고 있는 궤도에서 이탈하고 만다. 이러한 이탈의 방지가 이 작가에게서는 완벽을 기하고자 하는 철저한 조형성으로 나타나고 있다. 그리고 이 조형성이 오정희의 소설을 읽는 독자로 하여금 끊임없는 긴장을 요구하고 있다. 이 작가의 소설 미학의 요체라 할 수 있는 이러한 소설적 긴장은, 일상적인 삶에서 일어나는 사건들을 강조하거나 과장함으로써 독자들의 순간적인 쾌락을 만족시키는 상투적인 수법을 벗어나서, 소설이란 하나의 탐구라는 명제를 실현하고 있다. 아무 일도 일어나지 않는 일상적인 이야기인 것 같은 생각이 들 정

With Oh Jung-hee's stories, even a slightly careless reading of a word or expression can throw the reader off track. In an effort to prevent such misreadings, the author pays meticulous attention to molding a perfect narrative structure. This structural perfection is what forces us to be constantly on the alert. Indeed, the tension in Oh Jung-hee's narratives, the essence of her aesthetic, helps her stories transcend the hackneyed course of providing momentary pleasure by emphasizing or exaggerating everyday events, and instead fulfill the promise of fiction as an exploration of the unknown. If this lack of exaggeration causes her works to seem, on

도로 사건을 과장하지 않는 그의 소설은 그러나 바로 그 일상성 속에 자리 잡고 있는 비수의 번뜩임을 우리에게 감지하게 하고 있다.

김치수

하루 중에는 프랑스 사람들이 '개와 늑대 사이의 시간'이라고 부르는 시간이 있다. 해가 설핏 기울기 시작하고 땅거미가 내리면서 저만큼 보이는 짐승이 개인지 늑대인지 잘 분간이 가지 않는 미묘한 시간을 말함이다. 집에서 기르는 친숙한 가축이 문득 어두운 숲에서 내려오는 야생의 짐승처럼 낯설어 보이는 저 섬뜩한 시간, 그 '개와 늑대 사이의 시간'이 바로 오정희의 시간이다.

김화영

오정희의 소설들은 일상적 안정의 이면에서 위험스레 들끓는 무서운 에너지를 보여 준다. 그것은 운명일 수도 있고 사회적 어둠일 수도 있고 또는 자유와 욕망이라는 존재의 원초적인 에너지일 수도 있다. 오정희의 소설은 마지막의 경우에 보다 치중한다. 이 에너지는 일상의 안정을 파괴시키는 두려운 것이면서 동시에 삶을 이끌어가는 생명력이기도 하다. 오정희의 소설들은 이 에너지의

the surface, uneventful stories about ordinary life, it always allows the reader to sense the glint of a dagger buried in the very banality of existence.

Kim Chi-su

There is a time of day the French call the "time between the dog and the wolf." This is the hour, at sunset and dusk, when one cannot tell a dog from a wolf, when family pets or tame animals suddenly look unfamiliar, like wild beasts from a dark forest, and send chills up one's spine. This is the time that Oh Jung-hee explores and prowls in her fiction.

Kim Hwa-young

Oh Jung-hee's works allow us to glimpse the awesome energy that seethes perilously within everyday life. This energy may be seen as the force of human fate, the violence lurking in the dark side of society, or the exertion of free will and desire, two fundamentals of human existence. Oh's focus seems to be more on the forces of free will and desire, which can both destroy the stability of everyday life and infuse life with fresh vigor. In her stories, Oh talks about either the fear of such forces, or the shame of losing them while caught up in daily routines, or

분출이 지닌 두려움을 말하기도 하고, 일상의 테두리 속에서 이 에너지를 상실해 가는 부끄러움을 말하기도 하고, 또 이 두 가지 모순되는 사실이 빚어내는 삶의 본질적 비극성을 말하기도 한다. 이러한 것을 말함에 있어서 작가 오정희의 현실 투시력과 소설 구성력은 매우 뛰어나다. 그녀의 투시력은 아주 조그만 현실의 균열을 포착하여 그 사이로 이면에 숨어 있는 무서운 진실들을 끄집어낸다. 그리고 그것을 거의 완벽하게 소설로 재구성한다.

이남호

the tragedy caused by their dual nature. These narratives demonstrate her remarkable insights into reality and her ability to bring her novels practically to perfection. She discovers tiny cracks in the fabric of reality, extracts from them the dreadful truths hidden behind the facade, and rearranges them into an almost perfect fictional narrative.

Yi Nam-ho

오정희

작가 오정희는 1947년 서울에서 4남 4녀 중 다섯째로 태어났다. 그녀의 소설에 자주 등장하는 다산의 어머니는 아마도 작가 자신의 어머니에서 비롯된 것이 아닌가 싶다. 전쟁 때문에 황해도 해주에서 서울로, 서울에서 충청도 홍주까지 남하했던 오정희의 가족은, 1955년 4월 약 오 년간의 피난 생활을 정리하고 인천으로 이주했다가, 1959년 5월 아버지의 전근으로 다시 서울로 옮겨 간다. 피난지와 인천에서의 생활은 이후 「유년의 뜰」과 「중국인 거리」에서 소설로 형상화된다. 특히 인천은 중국인 마을과 양공주촌이 이웃에 있는 특이한 환경의 도시였는데 예민한 어린 소녀였던 오정희에게 이 시절은 독특한 기억으로 남는다. 오정희의 독서 경력은 열 살 때부터 본격화되었는데, 이때부터 오정희는 소설가를 꿈꾸게 된다. 인천 시절의 오정희는 별명이 쌈패, 싸움닭, 여맹위원장일 정도로 닥치는 대로 상대를 가리지 않고 달려들어 싸우면서 자기 얼굴, 남의 얼굴에 손톱 자국을 남기고 한 움큼씩 머

Oh Jung-hee

Oh Jung-hee was born as the fifth child among eight siblings—four boys and four girls—in 1947. The character of a mother who gives birth to many children, often featured in Oh's novels, might have been modeled after her own mother. Her family, which evacuated from Haeju, Hwanghae-do to Seoul and from Seoul to Hongju, Ch'ungchongnam-do during the Korean War, settled in Incheon in 1955, eventually moving to Seoul in 1959 when her father was relocated there for his work. Her experiences in the places of refuge and in Incheon were the basis of her stories, *Garden in My Childhood* and *Chinatown*. Especially, Incheon, in which Chinatown and "Foreigner's Whore Village" were in the neighborhood, left unique impressions on Oh's memory. Oh began devouring books and dreamed of becoming a writer at the age of ten. During this period, as illustrated in her nicknames such as hoodlum, gamecock, and committee chairwoman, Oh fought with anybody and everybody, scratching

리털을 뽑기도 했다. 심지어 초등학교 삼 학년 때 백일장에서 특선을 해서 시상식 날 아침 머리를 깎으러 이발소에 갔다가 이발사와 싸우느라 시상식에 참석을 못하기도 했다.

서울로 이주한 후, 오정희는 1960년 이화여자중학교에 입학하는데, 아버지의 권유로 정구부에 들어가 정구 선수 생활을 했다. 1963년에 이화여고에 입학하지만 학교에 잘 적응하지 못한 채, 몇 차례 가출을 감행하기도 한다. 1966년 서라벌 예술대학 문예창작과에 입학하고, 1968년 《중앙일보》 신춘문예에 「완구점 여인」이 당선되고 작가의 길에 들어선다. 첫 인터뷰 자리에서 가능하면 이름을 밝히지 않고 소설을 쓰고 싶다거나 청탁 받고 글 쓰는 일은 없을 것이라는 등의 말을 해서 담당 기자를 어리둥절하게 하기도 했다. 이는 아마도 상업적인 글은 쓰지 않겠다는 작가로서의 순결한 자기 맹세였던 것 같다. 등단 이후 잡지사, 출판사 등지로 직장을 전전하면서도 작품을 지속적으로 쓴다. 1974년 결혼, 그로부터 삼 년 후 첫 아이 정호를 출산하고 첫 창작집인 『불의 강』을 출간한다. 이듬해, 강원대학교에 전임강사로 임용된 남편을 따라 춘천으로 이주하여 지금까지 춘천에 거주하고 있다.

other people's faces or pulling a handful of their hair. On the day of an award ceremony, in which she was scheduled to receive the Special Selection Award for her entry in a writing contest as a third grader, she could not attend it because she fought with the barber, who was trimming her hair.

When she entered Ewha Girls Middle School in 1960, after Oh's family moved to Seoul, she was among the smallest in her class. She played tennis for a while on her father's advice. Although she entered Ewha Girls High School in 1963, she could not adjust to the school life very well and ran away from home a few times. After she entered the Creative Writing Program at Sŏrabŏl University of Art in 1966, she made her literary debut in 1968, as her short story "Toyshop Woman" won the *Joong-ang Ilbo* Spring Literary Contest. During her first interview she said that she wanted to publish stories incognito and that she wouldn't write just because she was asked to do, baffling the reporters. This was in fact the author's promise to herself that she wouldn't write simply to sell. She continued to write and publish stories while working for magazines and publishing companies. Three years after her marriage in 1974, she gave birth to her first child,

Jong-ho, and published her first collection of short stories, *River of Fire.* She moved to Chuncheon the next year, where she has been living ever since, as her husband got a position as full-time lecturer at Kangwon University.

번역 **브루스 풀턴** Translated by Bruce Fulton,
주찬 풀턴 Translated by Ju-chan Fulton

브루스 풀턴, 주찬 풀턴은 함께 한국문학 작품을 다수 영역해서 영미권에 소개하고 있다. 『별사-한국 여성 소설가 단편집』『여행자-한국 여성의 새로운 글쓰기』『유형의 땅』(공역, Marshall R. Pihl), 최윤의 소설집 『저기 소리 없이 한 점 꽃잎이 지고』, 황순원의 소설집 『잃어버린 사람들』『촛농 날개-악타 코리아나 한국 단편 선집』 외 다수의 작품을 번역하였다. 브루스 풀턴은 서울대학교 국어국문학과에서 박사 학위를 받고 캐나다의 브리티시컬럼비아 대학 민영빈 한국문학 및 문학 번역 교수로 재직하고 있다. 다수의 번역문학기금과 번역문학상 등을 수상한 바 있다.

Bruce and Ju-chan Fulton are the translators of several volumes of modern Korean fiction, including the award-winning women's anthologies *Words of Farewell: Stories by Korean Women Writers* (Seal Press, 1989) and *Wayfarer: New Writing by Korean Women* (Women in Translation, 1997), and with Marshall R. Pihl, *Land of Exile: Contemporary Korean Fiction*, rev. and exp. ed. (M.E. Sharpe, 2007). Their most recent translations are the 2009 Daesan Foundation Translation Award-winning *There a Petal Silently Falls: Three Stories by Ch'oe Yun* (Columbia University Press, 2008); *The Red Room: Stories of Trauma in Contemporary Korea* (University of Hawai'i Press, 2009), and *Lost Souls: Stories by Hwang Sunwŏn* (Columbia University Press, 2009). Bruce Fulton is co-translator (with Kim Chong-un) of *A Ready-Made Life: Early Masters of Modern Korean Fiction* (University of Hawai'i Press, 1998), co-editor (with Kwon Young-min) of *Modern Korean Fiction: An Anthology* (Columbia University Press, 2005), and editor of *Waxen Wings: The Acta Koreana Anthology of Short Fiction From Korea* (Koryo Press, 2011). The Fultons have received several awards and fellowships for their translations, including a National Endowment for the Arts Translation Fellowship, the first ever given for a translation from the Korean, and a residency at the Banff International Literary Translation Centre, the first ever awarded for translators from any Asian language. Bruce Fulton is the inaugural holder of the Young-Bin Min Chair in Korean Literature and Literary Translation, Department of Asian Studies, University of British Columbia. He is presently a Visiting Professor in the Department of Korean Language and Literature at the University of Seoul.

바이링궐 에디션 한국 대표 소설 011

중국인 거리

2012년 7월 25일 초판 1쇄 발행
2016년 7월 11일 초판 4쇄 펴냄

지은이 오정희 | **옮긴이** 브루스 풀턴, 주찬 풀턴 | **펴낸이** 김재범
감수 Bruce Fulton | **기획** 전성태, 정은경, 이경재
편집 김형욱, 윤단비 | **관리** 강초민
인쇄·제본 AP프린팅 | **종이** 한솔PNS
펴낸곳 ㈜아시아 | **출판등록** 2006년 1월 27일 제406-2006-000004호
주소 경기도 파주시 회동길 445(서울 사무소: 서울특별시 동작구 서달로 161-1 3층)
전화 02.821.5055 | **팩스** 02.821.5057 | **홈페이지** www.bookasia.org
ISBN 978-89-94006-20-8 (set) | 978-89-94006-31-4 (04810)
값은 뒤표지에 있습니다.

Bi-lingual Edition Modern Korean Literature 011

Chinatown

Written by Oh Jung-hee | **Translated by** Bruce and Ju-chan Fulton
Published by Asia Publishers | 445, heodong-gil, Paju-si, Gyeonggi-do, Korea
(Seoul Office: 161-1, Seodal-ro, Dongjak-gu, Seoul, Korea)
Homepage Address www.bookasia.org | **Tel.** (822).821.5055 | **Fax.** (822).821.5057
First published in Korea by Asia Publishers 2012
ISBN 978-89-94006-20-8 (set) | 978-89-94006-31-4 (04810)

바이링궐 에디션 한국 대표 소설

한국문학의 가장 중요하고 첨예한 문제의식을 가진 작가들의 대표작을 주제별로 선정!
하버드 한국학 연구원 및 세계 각국의 한국문학 전문 번역진이 참여한 번역 시리즈!
미국 하버드대학교와 컬럼비아대학교 동아시아학과, 캐나다 브리티시컬럼비아대학교 아시아학과 등 해외 대학에서 교재로 채택!

바이링궐 에디션 한국 대표 소설 set 1

분단 Division

01 병신과 머저리-**이청준** The Wounded-**Yi Cheong-jun**
02 어둠의 혼-**김원일** Soul of Darkness-**Kim Won-il**
03 순이삼촌-**현기영** Sun-i Samch'on-**Hyun Ki-young**
04 엄마의 말뚝 1-**박완서** Mother's Stake I-**Park Wan-suh**
05 유형의 땅-**조정래** The Land of the Banished-**Jo Jung-rae**

산업화 Industrialization

06 무진기행-**김승옥** Record of a Journey to Mujin-**Kim Seung-ok**
07 삼포 가는 길-**황석영** The Road to Sampo-**Hwang Sok-yong**
08 아홉 켤레의 구두로 남은 사내-**윤흥길** The Man Who Was Left as Nine Pairs of Shoes-**Yun Heung-gil**
09 돌아온 우리의 친구-**신상웅** Our Friend's Homecoming-**Shin Sang-ung**
10 원미동 시인-**양귀자** The Poet of Wŏnmi-dong-**Yang Kwi-ja**

여성 Women

11 중국인 거리-**오정희** Chinatown-**Oh Jung-hee**
12 풍금이 있던 자리-**신경숙** The Place Where the Harmonium Was-**Shin Kyung-sook**
13 하나코는 없다-**최윤** The Last of Hanak'o-**Ch'oe Yun**
14 인간에 대한 예의-**공지영** Human Decency-**Gong Ji-young**
15 빈처-**은희경** Poor Man's Wife-**Eun Hee-kyung**

바이링궐 에디션 한국 대표 소설 set 2

자유 Liberty

16 필론의 돼지-**이문열** Pilon's Pig-**Yi Mun-yol**
17 슬로우 불릿-**이대환** Slow Bullet-**Lee Dae-hwan**
18 직선과 독가스-**임철우** Straight Lines and Poison Gas-**Lim Chul-woo**
19 깃발-**홍희담** The Flag-**Hong Hee-dam**
20 새벽 출정-**방현석** Off to Battle at Dawn-**Bang Hyeon-seok**

사랑과 연애 Love and Love Affairs

21 별을 사랑하는 마음으로-**윤후명** With the Love for the Stars-**Yun Hu-myong**
22 목련공원-**이승우** Magnolia Park-**Lee Seung-u**
23 칼에 찔린 자국-**김인숙** Stab-**Kim In-suk**
24 회복하는 인간-**한강** Convalescence-**Han Kang**
25 트렁크-**정이현** In the Trunk-**Jeong Yi-hyun**

남과 북 South and North

26 판문점-**이호철** Panmunjom-**Yi Ho-chol**
27 수난 이대-**하근찬** The Suffering of Two Generations-**Ha Geun-chan**
28 분지-**남정현** Land of Excrement-**Nam Jung-hyun**
29 봄 실상사-**정도상** Spring at Silsangsa Temple-**Jeong Do-sang**
30 은행나무 사랑-**김하기** Gingko Love-**Kim Ha-kee**

바이링궐 에디션 한국 대표 소설 set 3

서울 Seoul

31 눈사람 속의 검은 항아리-**김소진** The Dark Jar within the Snowman-**Kim So-jin**
32 오후, 가로지르다-**하성란** Traversing Afternoon-**Ha Seong-nan**
33 나는 봉천동에 산다-**조경란** I Live in Bongcheon-dong-**Jo Kyung-ran**
34 그렇습니까? 기린입니다-**박민규** Is That So? I'm A Giraffe-**Park Min-gyu**
35 성탄특선-**김애란** Christmas Specials-**Kim Ae-ran**

전통 Tradition

36 무자년의 가을 사흘-**서정인** Three Days of Autumn, 1948-**Su Jung-in**
37 유자소전-**이문구** A Brief Biography of Yuja-**Yi Mun-gu**
38 향기로운 우물 이야기-**박범신** The Fragrant Well-**Park Bum-shin**
39 월행-**송기원** A Journey under the Moonlight-**Song Ki-won**
40 협죽도 그늘 아래-**성석제** In the Shade of the Oleander-**Song Sok-ze**

아방가르드 Avant-garde

41 아겔다마-**박상륭** Akeldama-**Park Sang-ryoong**
42 내 영혼의 우물-**최인석** A Well in My Soul-**Choi In-seok**
43 당신에 대해서-**이인성** On You-**Yi In-seong**
44 회색 時-**배수아** Time In Gray-**Bae Su-ah**
45 브라운 부인-**정영문** Mrs. Brown-**Jung Young-moon**

바이링궐 에디션 한국 대표 소설 set 4

디아스포라 Diaspora

46 속옷-**김남일** Underwear-**Kim Nam-il**
47 상하이에 두고 온 사람들-**공선옥** People I Left in Shanghai-**Gong Sun-ok**
48 모두에게 복된 새해-**김연수** Happy New Year to Everyone-**Kim Yeon-su**
49 코끼리-**김재영** The Elephant-**Kim Jae-young**
50 먼지별-**이경** Dust Star-**Lee Kyung**

가족 Family

51 혜자의 눈꽃-**천승세** Hye-ja's Snow-Flowers-**Chun Seung-sei**
52 아베의 가족-**전상국** Ahbe's Family-**Jeon Sang-guk**
53 문 앞에서-**이동하** Outside the Door-**Lee Dong-ha**
54 그리고, 축제-**이혜경** And Then the Festival-**Lee Hye-kyung**
55 봄밤-**권여선** Spring Night-**Kwon Yeo-sun**

유머 Humor

56 오늘의 운세-**한창훈** Today's Fortune-**Han Chang-hoon**
57 새-**전성태** Bird-**Jeon Sung-tae**
58 밀수록 다시 가까워지는-**이기호** So Far, and Yet So Near-**Lee Ki-ho**
59 유리방패-**김중혁** The Glass Shield-**Kim Jung-hyuk**
60 전당포를 찾아서-**김종광** The Pawnshop Chase-**Kim Chong-kwang**

바이링궐 에디션 한국 대표 소설 set 5

관계 Relationship

61 도둑견습 - **김주영** Robbery Training-**Kim Joo-young**
62 사랑하라, 희망 없이 - **윤영수** Love, Hopelessly-**Yun Young-su**
63 봄날 오후, 과부 셋 - **정지아** Spring Afternoon, Three Widows-**Jeong Ji-a**
64 유턴 지점에 보물지도를 묻다 - **윤성희** Burying a Treasure Map at the U-turn-**Yoon Sung-hee**
65 쁘이거나 쯔이거나 - **백가흠** Puy, Thuy, Whatever-**Paik Ga-huim**

일상의 발견 Discovering Everyday Life

66 나는 음식이다 - **오수연** I Am Food-**Oh Soo-yeon**
67 트럭 - **강영숙** Truck-**Kang Young-sook**
68 통조림 공장 - **편혜영** The Canning Factory-**Pyun Hye-young**
69 꽃 - **부희령** Flowers-**Pu Hee-ryoung**
70 피의일요일 - **윤이형** Bloody Sunday-**Yun I-hyeong**

금기와 욕망 Taboo and Desire

71 북소리 - **송영** Drumbeat-**Song Yong**
72 발칸의 장미를 내게 주었네 - **정미경** He Gave Me Roses of the Balkans-**Jung Mi-kyung**
73 아무도 돌아오지 않는 밤 - **김숨** The Night Nobody Returns Home-**Kim Soom**
74 젓가락여자 - **천운영** Chopstick Woman-**Cheon Un-yeong**
75 아직 일어나지 않은 일 - **김미월** What Has Yet to Happen-**Kim Mi-wol**

바이링궐 에디션 한국 대표 소설 set 6

운명 Fate

76 언니를 놓치다 - **이경자** Losing a Sister-**Lee Kyung-ja**
77 아들 - **윤정모** Father and Son-**Yoon Jung-mo**
78 명두 - **구효서** Relics-**Ku Hyo-seo**
79 모독 - **조세희** Insult-**Cho Se-hui**
80 화요일의 강 - **손홍규** Tuesday River-**Son Hong-gyu**

미의 사제들 Aesthetic Priests

81 고수 - **이외수** Grand Master-**Lee Oisoo**
82 말을 찾아서 - **이순원** Looking for a Horse-**Lee Soon-won**
83 상춘곡 - **윤대녕** Song of Everlasting Spring-**Youn Dae-nyeong**
84 삭매와 자미 - **김별아** Sakmae and Jami-**Kim Byeol-ah**
85 저만치 혼자서 - **김훈** Alone Over There-**Kim Hoon**

식민지의 벌거벗은 자들 The Naked in the Colony

86 감자 - **김동인** Potatoes-**Kim Tong-in**
87 운수 좋은 날 - **현진건** A Lucky Day-**Hyŏn Chin'gŏn**
88 탈출기 - **최서해** Escape-**Ch'oe So-hae**
89 과도기 - **한설야** Transition-**Han Seol-ya**
90 지하촌 - **강경애** The Underground Village-**Kang Kyŏng-ae**

바이링궐 에디션 한국 대표 소설 set 7

백치가 된 식민지 지식인 Colonial Intellectuals Turned "Idiots"

91 날개 - **이상** Wings-**Yi Sang**
92 김 강사와 T 교수 - **유진오** Lecturer Kim and Professor T-**Chin-O Yu**
93 소설가 구보씨의 일일 - **박태원** A Day in the Life of Kubo the Novelist-**Pak Taewon**
94 비 오는 길 - **최명익** Walking in the Rain-**Ch'oe Myŏngik**
95 빛 속에 - **김사량** Into the Light-**Kim Sa-ryang**

한국의 잃어버린 얼굴 Traditional Korea's Lost Faces

해방 전후(前後) Before and After Liberation

전후(戰後) Korea After the Korean War